THE PHYSICS
OF GRIEF

Other titles by Mickey J. Corrigan

THE PHYSICS OF GRIEF

a novel by

Mickey J. Corrigan

POISONED
CHALICE

Poisoned Chalice
An imprint of QuoScript
71-75 Shelton Road, London WC2H 9JQ, United Kingdom

www.quoscript.co.uk

This paperback edition 2021

A CIP catalogue record for this book is available from
the British Library

Typeset in Adobe Garamond Pro

ISBN: 978-1-8382672-0-9 (paperback edition)
ISBN: 978-1-8382930-9-3 (electronic edition)

This book is dedicated to everyone grieving a loss.
Owing to the global ravages of the 2020 pandemic,
a full accounting of our losses is unimaginable.
Our grief, however, is shared.

Preface

IN 2004, STEPHEN Hawking announced that for the past thirty years he had been wrong about black hole theory. After the famous physicist made his theoretical mistake in 1976, scientists puzzled over the paradox of black hole information retrieval. Finally, Hawking resolved the paradox he had created.

The celebrated physicist from the University of Cambridge was the author of the book *A Brief History of Time*, which sold more than ten million copies worldwide. Quantum physics, also known as New Physics, is based on scientific laws that state unequivocally how information can never be lost. Stephen Hawking's earlier research indicated that black holes, the collapsed stars which absorb nearby light and matter, do not allow the retrieval of such information, but only emit radiation. Newer research, however, indicated black holes not only emit radiation but, at the same time, reveal information from within. To the great satisfaction of theoretical scientists everywhere, Hawking corroborated the quantum laws, postulating that in our world and beyond *nothing is ever lost.*

In a speech given on a college campus in 2009, Hawking pointed to the scientific evidence which supported the idea that if one fell into a black hole one could emerge in a wholly different universe. Hawking continued to publicize his revamped theory, reiterating that black holes were not the eternal prisons he once believed; and he maintained this position until his death in 2018.

So, what does this mean for the rest of us? It means this: whenever something dies – a star, a memory, a loved one – it is not lost. Hawking's theory means that whatever dies to us is still in existence somewhere else. This means our longing over impossible distances, across space and across time, may on some unknown level have impact and import.

It means we know nothing about the meaning of death.

Or life, for that matter.

Be grateful I'm telling you this now. I learned about such matters the hard way after I lost someone dear to me. Ignorant and afraid, I led a half-life for years, a depressed loser unable to pull myself out of the black hole of my grief. But my worldview was altered dramatically when I became a professional griever.

This is why I want to share that story with you.

Seymour Patrick Allan
Spring, 2022

My Wasteland Life

M Y SEAT BY the window allowed a view of the dirty street, bright and ugly in the merciless glare of the sun. Hollywood had been baking all morning in its own juices, simmering too long under the emotional pressure of being the unknown Hollywood, the starless Hollywood with no famous film studios, the bland suburban Hollywood a few miles north of glittery Miami.

Every once in a while the coffee shop manager, a chubby and jolly man wrapped tightly in a butcher's apron, announced something jovial in Spanish. Then some of the patrons would chuckle.

There was a kind of café din, the bustling sound of people talking and laughing, dishes clattering, coffee spoons clinking against chipped cups and saucers, chairs scraping across loose tiles, traffic outside making itself known. But the din at La Cantina was in reality a coffee shop din, not a café din, and I had to admit this to myself. This was South Florida, not Paris. Not New York, not even my hometown, Boston.

I was nowhere and I knew it.

Ignoring the cold dregs of my last cup of coffee, I tried to focus on the crossword puzzle in front of me. Retired people, doddering fools of about my age, were supposed to find such puzzles mentally stimulating. But boredom had long ago gelled in my gut and I could feel it trembling slightly like old flan. Chewing what was left of my pencil, I stared at the empty little squares and pictured Marnie with her red dress over her head.

"Excuse me. May I ask you something?"

And suddenly there he was, just like in a dream. A tall pale man seated directly across my little round table for two. The man's eyes glittered behind rimless glasses. He wore no mask to protect himself from the virus and his mouth pursed itself girlishly. When he moved he barely made a sound. His coffee cup was tiny, a ceramic shot of espresso which he downed silently, swiftly.

"I hope I'm not interrupting anything," the man said, wiping his thin lips with a paper napkin in a depressing shade of recycled brown. "I've seen you in here a few times this week and . . . if I may be frank? You look like you need something to do. It just so happens I have a bit of work that might interest you."

His lips smiled while his eyes stared out coldly from some unknowable interior space. I waved a hand in front of him to make him disappear, but he remained seated across from me, unruffled. He was closer to me than the six feet regulation allowed, but that didn't faze me. At this point in my life, an early visit from the grim reaper would've been welcome.

"Shall I tell you about the job?" he asked.

His solicitous demeanor gave me the kind of creeps I got around priests and undertakers. For good reason, it turned out. The man slid his business card across the stained formica table, gently skirting my crossword puzzle book. *Raymond C. Dasher, Professional Grievers, Inc.* was printed on a laminated white card with a local phone number in the same basic block font.

As I studied the card, a stampede of thunderclouds approached, announcing themselves with a dramatic overture. Behind Raymond, the fat-faced manager swirled one index finger in the air to indicate another round of coffee was on the way. I shrugged because I would certainly drink more if the coffee was free. Raymond nodded. He'd assumed correctly I would be willing to listen to his pitch if my drink was refreshed.

"Here's how it works," Raymond said after the hot coffee had been served and the masked manager waddled away. "My service is unique, and I have built my reputation on the promise of complete discretion. My clients come to me reluctantly when they are desperate for help, desperate enough to pay top dollar for my services. And with what do I provide them? I provide them with peace of mind at a time of utmost vulnerability. I provide them with a means of exiting the stage to a standing ovation. A way to say farewell with the kind of royal fanfare they think they deserve. Especially now that funerals are less populated. In the modern era, virus or no virus, we should give the dying whatever they desire. Don't you agree?"

He looked to me for approval, so I stared back at him noncommittally. Raymond appeared to be around my age or a little older, maybe sixty, but his baby face had few wrinkles, only a spattering of sun damage freckles. His accent was neither New York nor foreign, a rare treat in South Florida. Nobody here is from here. Everyone is from Long Island, Cuba, or someplace else distinctively other.

Rain spattered the window beside us. A baby squall: it wouldn't last long. I glanced out at the changing street scene. Umbrellas had popped open, people were hunched and scurrying, and the buff drug dealers drifted away from the corner toward a convenience store with a broad green and white striped awning. The coffee shop windows were fogging up as the front door opened and closed repeatedly, soaked stragglers ducking inside to escape the sudden downpour.

I wasn't that interested in the stranger's pitch, but I sipped my free cup of coffee and urged the man across from me to carry on talking. A distraction appealed. Life had dulled for me, dulling even more during the long months of the virus and, if nothing else, this stranger in my personal space served as a welcome distraction.

Raymond glanced around us at the raucous crowd and smiled

in a patronizing way before he continued to pontificate. "In Nigeria when a relative dies you shave your head and refuse to answer the telephone. Can you imagine anyone in our society willing to make such a sacrifice? In certain Australian tribes after the death of a spouse the widow never speaks again. She uses sign language for the rest of her life. No American wife would ever consider shutting up to mourn the loss of her husband." He shook his head in disapproval.

When thunder exploded overhead, I jumped in my seat. Raymond remained motionless. His hands lay like dead fish on the table, ringless and white as candle wax. He kept talking, his eyes on mine, while car alarms screeched and more people pushed inside the storefront to escape the storm. He was completely unruffled.

"The Canadian Ojibwa would pour ashes on their heads after a loved one died, and the men pushed knives, needles, or thorns through the skin of their chests and arms. The LoDagaa of Ghana are said to bind up the relatives of the deceased in order to restrain their grief. Many cultures once buried alive those closest to the recently departed. Women and slaves were walled up in tombs, some with a view of the church conducting the funeral. Victorians dressed in black and behaved like living monuments to the dead for years afterward."

Raymond's steel grey eyes felt like fingers prodding the skin on my face. I stared back, emboldened by his complete lack of stranger distance. When he smiled his teeth looked too wide and heavy for his narrow jaw. He was ugly but suave. His suit was impeccable and made of something expensive. I reminded myself to check out his shoes when he stood up. I was thinking Italian leather and perfectly shined.

"In our highly advanced culture, we have little time or inclination to mourn the dead," he said. "Most Americans slip in and out of wakes quickly on their way home from work. We have our assistants send flowers, we email condolences in between shopping trips or business meetings. Death is neatly, cleanly removed from us by the modern hospital, the high-tech funeral business, the abstraction of a crematorium or pre-dug gravesite at an anonymous cemetery. No fuss, no muss. Not much need for us to ever feel emotionally involved. Especially now, when keeping one's distance is strongly recommended by our medical experts."

Raymond eyed the crowded café, scanning the few patrons in masks. The coffee shop manager wore a thick double mask. He circled, waiting to come in for the kill. He wanted his table back. When he flapped the check at me, I waved him away.

Raymond went on. "In the West, the separation of the living from the dying increases with every new generation. We hide our dying in medical buildings and allow advanced technology to dictate what we do for them and how long we do it for. No wonder Americans prefer quick deaths that arrive without warning. In other cultures, the people appreciate a slow death that allows loved ones to come visit and the dying to make proper arrangements. Death is seen as an important part of the life cycle, an opportunity to learn essential life lessons. Everyone wishes to be present for the death of a loved one. And the funeral is a rite of passage, another important step in the journey. No one wants to miss out on it."

I couldn't help myself, I started thinking of Marnie naked, her thin auburn hair draped across her soft pink breasts, the way she reached for me hungrily. I blew my nose into my handkerchief and folded it carefully, returning it to my shorts pocket.

Raymond leaned in. "Excuse me for my frankness, but I sense in you a compassion for others. And an acute loneliness, a desire for companionship. Am I correct?"

He smoothed his faded hair with one hand in a gesture that could be seen as vain but which I recognized as humility. A sensitive man. That was, after all, his business.

He could see I was the sensitive type, too. So I nodded. Okay, he had me pegged.

He sat back. "Because in my line of work one has to be a selective judge of character. I don't approach everybody with an offer of work, believe me. I must sense something quite special in the person's character before I am willing to consider them for the job."

I decided to ask a few questions, beginning with the obvious. How much to do what, and when and where.

"Let me explain more about the generalities first," Raymond replied, "and then we will get to the particulars."

The windows rapidly defogged. The rain had cooled off the streets and cleaned away the sweat and grime. When the sun came out again the asphalt would gleam. The palm trees lining Hollywood Boulevard were still flailing in a gusty wind, but the storm had sizzled out. The coffee shop quieted down as customers ventured back into the humid afternoon air.

"There are a lot of lonely people in the world," Raymond said, and his eyes wandered around the room again. Most of the tables were occupied by single folks. An elderly man in baggy, dirt-brown shorts. A grandmother type wearing a bulky yellow cardigan to ward off the air conditioning. A scrawny fellow who looked like he could use a good meal. A middle-aged fat guy who looked like he'd had too many good meals. All of these people looked emptied out.

I probably looked the same way.

"Here in South Florida, a lot of people are sitting around, waiting to die. And guess what," Raymond continued, his wan face serene. "It's inevitable that all of them will indeed die. Not all at once, not all from the virus, please don't misunderstand me. What I am saying is, no one wishes to die alone, to be buried anonymously or cremated without farewells, to be instantly forgotten. We admire those who die spectacularly and earn thousands of mourners. Like Princess Diana. President Kennedy. Elvis. John Lewis. Unfortunately, in a society that avoids the dying and hides itself from the mundane realities of death, many people have end-of-life desires that are left unfulfilled."

I could see that. Wakes and funerals were regarded by some as potential super-spreader events, a good excuse for avoiding them. Meanwhile, the bars and cafés were busier than ever. And as for end of life desires, my own later years were turning out to be much more disappointing than I'd expected.

Raymond cleared his throat, leaned in again. "You can understand how there would be any number of lonely people in South Florida with more money than loved ones willing to attend a funeral. Well, it turns out that some of these people are willing to pay strangers to come to their bedside or graveside and mourn their passing." He touched the business card lying next to my coffee cup with an icy-looking index finger. "It is my business to facilitate such events. And right now, business is hopping."

At some point the coffee shop manager had dropped the tab on the table. Even though several other tables had been freed up, the manager was evil-eyeing me now from his post behind the cash register. Usually he let me sit for as long as I cared to. Since I remained quiet and tipped well, my lingering was part of our unspoken agreement. I wasn't sure why he seemed so agitated now, so anxious to see me go.

Perhaps sensing my discomfort, Raymond reached for his wallet. The long leather billfold was absolutely stuffed with cash. Without looking at me, he asked, "Would you be willing to come to my office and discuss the details of working for me? The job is freelance, so you would be employed on a case by case basis."

Before I could respond, he reached out, handing me two crisp hundreds. "I'd like you to get started this afternoon."

My retirement had been more or less forced. More, actually, so I was always down on funds. Way down. Living small. So how could I say no?

When I accepted the money he smiled and nodded his pleasure. Then we stood up. Raymond towered over me. I tend to stoop and creep, which serves to accentuate my downbeat personality.

"Shall we? My office is close by," Raymond ordered from his dual position of height and financial advantage.

I would follow my new boss, I decided, and see where it took me.

For most of my life I'd shied away from funerals. And death. The emptiness, the infinite bleakness seemed too morose, so dangerously attractive for a depressive like myself. Then Marnie died and I was instantly overwhelmed by unresolvable loss, the finality of life's meaninglessness. The lethal virus had served to enhance my gloomy perspective. With this job, however, I could look at death differently: death would provide me with an income.

My monochrome existence ached for a change of scene. Fewer crossword puzzles, more . . . I wasn't sure, but it would most certainly be different than what I could find sitting at a little table at La Cantina.

"I'm Seymour Allan," I told Raymond. "I live right down the street. Emerald Day Village. It's a retirement community for active adults."

"Yes, I know," he said, and tossed a newly minted twenty-dollar bill on the table.

I contemplated the coffee-stained crossword puzzle book lying on the café table, now with a clean green twenty on top of it. A lovely tableau, a kind of before and after portrait of my wasteland life.

Raymond said, "We create our lives from one moment to the next."

Later, at his office, he would explain the comment. As it turned out, this was the First Rule of Professional Grievers. There were ten of these rules. I was to memorize them and try to understand how they shaped my role as a professional griever.

But I didn't know that yet.

Feeling mildly positive for a change, I followed him to the door. He opened it for us, and we headed into the blast furnace outside. The sudden humidity was shocking to the system, but typical of South Florida, so I was used to it. Raymond seemed unaffected by it, too.

As I fell into step beside him, I glanced down at my new employer's size thirteen feet. Sure enough, Raymond wore a pair of very expensive-looking Italian leather shoes.

And they were shined to perfection.

Coffee Spoons I

Before we continue, let's put all our coffee spoons on the table.

You probably don't want to know that much about me. Admit it. You don't care about my unhappy childhood, my mediocre education in the public school system, my half-assed college degree and the long years of low-wage work. Who cares that I missed too much time on the job and faced an embarrassing forced retirement before I turned fifty? You'll simply stop reading if I start in on the ex-wife and her infertility issues, how my drinking and screwing around ruined us and, least interesting of all, my excuses for being such a loser. You'll stop listening and click on your favorite YouTube videos or Instagram feeds if I bore you by whining about my past.

I mean, I get it. You're more interested in the action. The plot line and how fast it takes you to the sex, the boozing, the mobsters, the continued downward spiral of a man's life. You want to feel better in comparison. After all, how bad could your life be – a poor career choice, maybe, the one brief affair, a couple nights of drunkenness here and there? All that is child's play compared to *my* bad choices, right?

So, enough about me. I won't bother with the details of my life before Raymond C. Dasher. I didn't bother Raymond with the ho-hum particulars, either. He seemed to have all the information he needed anyway. There were no forms to fill out at

Professional Grievers, Inc., no drug tests or insurance information was required. No references from former employers or landlords. He didn't do a background check on me. No credit check. He didn't ask me if I owned or rented my home. He knew by looking at me exactly where I was coming from and what it would take to get me to somewhere else.

To sun-beaten cemeteries and dark funeral homes, to the houses of strangers, to the inside of elaborate churches and small chapels. To the bedside and the graveside of the deeply unloved. To the heart of death – strangers' deaths and my own.

But I admit it: I didn't do any vetting either. After meeting Raymond at La Cantina, I didn't look up Professional Grievers, Inc., on the Internet to see if they were a licensed corporation in the state of Florida. I didn't ask around to find out what kind of a reputation this oddball with the creepy business had around town. I was so damn tired of my lame lonely existence that I simply accepted the man's offer of money in exchange for my time. I was willing to sell whatever time I had left to a stranger, it was that worthless to me.

Maybe you know the feeling. Maybe not. Either way, I should tell you this. Wisdom is not available to us while we mope around in the land of the living. It just isn't. You can only find wisdom when you're good as dead. When you have nothing left to lose. When it's all over but the dying.

And let me say this about death. Everything we think we are will be demolished. That's all we know, all we *can* know. Maybe we don't have any background information to prop us up. Maybe we don't have all the scientific facts or spiritual guidelines we think we'll need. So what? Tough shit. Death is *here*. Death is waiting for us every step of the way on our individual life journeys, and we must deal with it – head on, face to face – on our own final day. And on the final days of those we love.

There's really no way around death. And that's all there is to know about it.

If I had to summarize for you my life before I met Raymond C. Dasher, I'd say it was dull and largely disappointing. There were a few high points, but mostly I fucked things up. Not royally, no. Just regularly. Enough so that I hated myself. Enough so that sitting around at other people's wakes and funerals sounded like a better way to spend my time than sitting around with my own half-dead self.

This is how I became an employee (freelance, on a case by case basis) of Professional Grievers, Inc.

April

M Y FIRST GRIEF case was that very afternoon. I was nervous, but the job was okay. Easy work, unsettling work.
I attended the funeral of a stranger, where I wept quietly in a
semi-full pew, and again in a too-close throng by the open grave.
I didn't attempt to connect with any of the other mourners, all of
whom were masked, as was I. And I didn't push my way to the
front to toss a handful of dirt on the coffin after it was lowered
into its fresh and sanitary-looking hole. I did manage to speak to
the widow for a moment before the crowd in black pressed in. Part
of my job description.

"I'm sorry for your loss," I recited in a muffled voice, my eyes
lowered. This was what I had been instructed (paid) to say. "He
was a generous man and made a deep impact on me." This was
improvisation.

The widow, fortyish and built like a barmaid from a tough part
of town, stared at me for a moment. Then she let out a hollow
laugh. I tore my eyes from the ponderous cleavage stuffed inside
her stiff black blouse to look into a pair of surprisingly clear eyes.

"You gotta be shittin' me," she said in a nicotine-flavored voice.
"He give you the time of day? Not me, the motherfucker."

Second Rule of Professional Grievers, according to Raymond:
It is not possible to be of any real use to others.

Raymond had recited his list of rules before sending me
off on this first assignment. I'd listened, nodded, but I did not

understand. Over time, however, my work as a professional griever would teach me the validity of each of Raymond's rules.

Feeling scorned by the widow, I moved aside to allow the other mourners to address her in her time of loss. She seemed amused by the people and their stumbling words of sympathy. A few times she croaked out a boisterous laugh.

Her attitude aside, the work went smoothly. Getting paid so much money for such a simple and brief job seemed like a hand-out, however. I liked professional grieving right away, it suited me, but I couldn't understand why I'd been hired. There were at least fifty people in attendance at that first funeral job, which was over the viral limit at the time. People didn't seem to care. They were of all ages, shapes, and sizes. Trim young women with babies, old men with rusted walkers, teenagers with ear buds and bored expressions. Was everyone there on the payroll of Professional Grievers, Inc.? If so, what was *I* needed for?

Most likely nothing. But I carried out my minor unobtrusive role as instructed. Then I slipped away.

On the short drive home, my mask hanging from the rearview mirror, I pondered. The job made no sense to me. Two hundred dollars for a few hours sitting quietly in a cool dark church and standing respectfully under a canvas canopy on the rolling lawn of the city cemetery. Two hundred bucks in advance, just for pre-tending to be sad. And it wasn't an act, I didn't have to pretend. The weeping was real. All I had to do was think about Marnie with her opalesque acrylic fingernails, the way she'd hold my tired head in her soft lap, gently scratching my scalp and whisper-ing, "You're my one and only. It'll all be fine. Don't worry, baby."

After several more funerals, each one providing both two hundred dollars in cash *and* the appropriate setting for a cathartic weeping session, Raymond assigned me to a bigger case. Over the phone, he warned me this one would require a much larger investment of my time.

"Pre-death grief cases include bedside mourning for as long as it takes. Plus the wake, the funeral, and graveside attendance. The rate is two thousand dollars. A thousand in advance and the rest on completion. Plus a bonus."

I was fist-pumping on my end of the phone line until Raymond said the bonus depended on some factors that seemed entirely vague to me.

"Can you explain more clearly what I'll need to do to earn the bonus?" I asked him, while pouring coffee into a chipped mug in my sunlit kitchen. I yawned deeply. I'd overslept, forgetting I was now employed. "You didn't tell me I'd be working with the undead," I added.

Raymond said not to worry, the dying man did not have the virus. "It's cancer," he said. "End stage."

Not that I would say no. Who was I to turn down two thousand bucks? And I wasn't trying all that hard to avoid contracting the virus. My depression was teetering on suicidal.

"We'll see how you do on this case." Raymond refused to elucidate on the bonus. "Case by case basis" was all he would say.

On my way to the gig, I dropped by the office so Raymond could pay me the advance. Cash, always cash. This did not seem bona fide to me, but I wasn't about to complain. A few days' grief work was legions better than crossword puzzles and coffee dregs. Raymond kept the instructions brief, reminding me about the Ten Rules and handing me a printout with directions to the client's house.

On my way to the parking lot I took a look at where I would be going for the gig. *Shit.* Boca fucking Raton? I was tempted to return to the office and hand him back the money, but I swallowed my bile and climbed into my beaten Toyota with the peeling orange paint. I hated my ugly car. More than that, I hated the idea of my car in Boca Raton. Because I hated everything that wealthy, snobby, phony city stood for.

But two thousand bucks was two thousand bucks. So, with a bitter taste in my mouth, I started up my car and headed for I-95.

~

Raymond had said it might take a few days. Maybe a week, including the burial ceremonies. But his estimates for the length of service on the new case were wildly inaccurate. A month after I collected my advance at his office, I was still on duty. I was still at the dying client's house in tony Boca Raton. I was still a professional griever, but I was not doing any grieving.

The case was still active, but so was the client. In fact, the client was more active than *I* was. More active than I'd *ever been*.

I wanted to go home, but the client wouldn't let me. The job Raymond had assigned me to had no foreseeable end. I was trapped in the city of my nightmares.

Every few days I checked in with Raymond. At first I kept him informed of the client's health status, but eventually I began to beg for help. The client, the guy who hired Professional Grievers, Inc., in order to make his death seem like a big deal, this guy seemed to really like me. He said he wanted me to stick around. Indefinitely. He told me he wasn't gung-ho on dying anymore. He'd lost the urge. No more *I'm on my way outs*. Lots of *we oughta go to Vegas* (or Palm Springs, or the Turks and Caicos).

You get the picture.

With each call, Raymond said the same thing. He advised me to hang in. Do the work. Finish the case. He didn't seem worried that the job could go on and on until finally *I* was the one who keeled over.

Eventually Raymond showed up in Boca, inviting me out for coffee and a pep talk.

"You don't get it," I told him with a frown, while Raymond stared back at me, placid as ever.

We were seated outside an Italian market a block west of the client's oceanfront home, in the shade of a large yellow and pink SunFest umbrella. We were alone on the patio, the other customers preferring to stay inside in the comfort of air conditioning. We sipped our espressos.

"This is not a job for a professional griever anymore, Raymond. I need you to let me off the case."

The day was hot and damp, the spring rain holding itself back, teasing like a virgin. In the dappled sunlight the psychedelic spurts of orange and purple bougainvillea decorating the white marble shopping plaza doorways were vividly impressionistic. The town itself was a thing of conflicting beauty. Landscaped in a kind of choked wildness, it reeked of expensive manicure and dirty capital. Living in Boca Raton was psychic torture. I was way out of my element. Compared to Emerald Day Village, it was a big step up for me. *A real reach,* Marnie would've said.

"He's not sick anymore. He's healthier than I am," I told Raymond.

The client was off his deathbed with a vengeance. In fact, at this moment he was playing tennis at his private club with the twenty-something pro. After tennis, he'd told me that morning, he would bike home and swim laps in his infinity pool.

Raymond patted his lips with a linen napkin. We both watched as a stunning young woman sauntered past. She wore only a lime-colored bikini, the miniscule bottom resembling a stripper's G-string, and a pair of sparkling red heels. A three-foot iguana was draped around her neck. The iguana emitted a neon orange glow and I swear the thing was grinning at us. *Look at this, I'm a frigging reptile and I'm the one with the hot babe*, it seemed to be saying.

Anything beat being an old guy.

I told Raymond the backstory I'd heard from our client. When diagnosed with advanced prostate cancer, Milton Lasker had reacted badly, refusing to undergo the recommended surgery. He sought more opinions. Five Harvard-trained oncologists in a row warned him he would not survive unless he followed their instructions. "I'll die then," Mr Lasker had said. "But with my pecker intact. I'll go out fucking – and I don't mean gentle into that fucking night. I'm a fan of the Dylan Thomas school of dying," he shouted at the doctors one by one as he traveled the U.S. in search of a more acceptable diagnosis.

He couldn't find one, so eventually he gave up. By then it was too late for surgery. So he hired Raymond and got me, the neophyte bedside griever.

Raymond stared at me, waiting for the punch line. There wasn't one. I'd fucked up the job, and maybe a miracle had occurred.

I hemmed for a moment, then blurted, "It's all my fault." I paused, regaining control of myself. "The thing is, even though Mr Lasker was dying when I first got here, he was still so full of life. This guy has *really* lived, Raymond. And he's hungry for more. He just doesn't want it to end."

Unlike me with my major downer, who-cares, life-sucks attitude.

They say opposites attract. Not that I was attracted to the man. I didn't swing that way, never had. However, his attitude absolutely intoxicated me. And I was a sucker for intoxicants. I was enthralled by the way he took what was not his, and cleanly dismissed what he no longer had use for. All *without a speck of guilt.*

Mr Lasker made the best of his wasteland. I'd never met anyone so cool and self-accepting. I was mesmerized.

Employing my superpower of fuck-it-up thinking, I decided Mr Lasker deserved more than a lonely goodbye. I didn't want a man like that to die quietly, a paid griever by the bed and an anonymous crowd of extras at the funeral. So I talked him out of dying. I brought him hope. Paperbacks on nutrition and healing. A juicer and bags of fresh veggies. I even got the local reiki master to come by.

Not that I was a believer in alternative care and voodoo cures. I just thought it would be good for the man not to give up. Not yet. Of course, this unilateral decision was above my pay grade. I was entirely out of my element on that as well.

Raymond's Third Rule of Professional Grievers: All our knowledge reveals the extent of our true ignorance. I could see that. And, ultimately, how this ignorance would bring us down the road to our death. But it wasn't working in this case. Not with Mr Lasker.

"He says he's planning to live forever," I told Raymond, setting aside my empty espresso cup.

The humidity was stifling. Raymond appeared unbothered by it, not a drop of perspiration on his forehead. However, he did remove his baby blue Armani suit coat. Then he continued to sit silently across from me, inscrutable behind his mirrored shades.

I sweated and cringed in the uncomfortable wrought-iron chair, embarrassed at the role I'd played in reviving our client. "He thinks it's really gonna happen. Because of the raw diet, the reiki. Plus, you told me to read to him on his deathbed. And Mr Lasker really liked the stuff I read to him. I guess it gave him inspiration. The inspiration to *live*."

I'd started with Gerald Stern, Philip Levine, a handful of my favorite poets in a textbook collection I'd brought with me. But it was Allen Ginsberg who made Mr Lasker sit up and smile. Who knew radical Jewish fervor laced with New Age food-faddism would get the old guy's juices flowing again?

I knew I was responsible for the situation. My bad. Now Lasker's indebtedness had paralyzed me. I needed to move on but I couldn't.

I looked at Raymond for a sign he was angry, or possibly forgiving. There was none. He was like an ice sculpture. I needed to get a rise out of him, force him to scold me and let the air out of my guilt balloon.

I sat back in the chair. In a high-toned Boca Raton snob tone, I said, "Ginsberg's social discourse isn't one of those in which we inscribe ourselves in the sentimental narrative. But Mr Lasker processed the subtext in his own way, and now he's decided to be immortal."

This was actually said in more of an intellectual Boston snob tone; but it did elicit a response.

Raymond sighed loudly. He removed his designer shades. Without his glasses he looked tired. He pinched the bridge of his thin nose carefully before speaking. I could tell he was annoyed with me and my petty snobbery, my silly attitude toward the serious job at hand.

"Seymour, we are in the grieving business. Not the hope business. We leave hope to the politicians and the salespeople, the advertisers and the film studios. They have the hope market covered. We, on the other hand, provide our clients with the support they need to get through the final act in the human script. We allow our clients to die in the company of others and to be remembered as popular and well loved. Even if they were not. *Especially* if they were not. This is what we are paid to do. Death is our business. If our clients don't die, then we aren't able to do our job. Do you understand what I'm saying?"

I nodded. My stomach felt tight. I was such a fuckup I couldn't even help a dying guy die.

Raymond put his sunglasses back on and crossed his long arms. "The Javanese believe it is the dead who can provide the living with an ideal image of proper behavior: still, aloof, unengaged nothingness. Nonbeingness. Can you imagine Americans striving toward such a selfless self-image?"

I shifted in the hard chair. I was uncomfortable, and my shorts were giving me a wedgie. Mr Lasker had purchased some new clothes for me. He'd informed me I was not properly dressed to go out in Boca and in need of a dramatic makeover. The pastel Bermuda shorts and Hawaiian fat-guy shirts he bought me were high-ticket Boca Country Club clothes. But in reality I was more of a Pompano Dog Track kind of guy.

I was costumed for a role I didn't want to play.

While I was fingering the silk collar of my floral shirt and trying to think of some sort of response, Raymond leaned forward. In a stern voice he advised, "Watch your step with this case. You need to remain professional so you can earn out your freelance fee. And bonus."

He was right. But at this point I wanted to forget about the money and crawl home to Emerald Day Village.

He took pity on me. "You're new at grieving. A greenhorn at death. So keep at it. Do the work. Finish the case. Earn your fee, Seymour."

Good advice. Too bad I was unmotivated. I didn't want to try to convince Mr Lasker he was mortal. I didn't want the guy to die.

A few days after Raymond's visit I drove Mr Lasker in his jet black Mercedes sports coupé to one of the many impeccable golf courses in that ridiculously impeccable city. Then I drove the electric cart while Mr Lasker played golf. Or more accurately I retrieved the balls the client hit into landscaped scrub brush and sand traps. The late afternoon sun seared our scalps through our thinning hair and sweat dripped from our craggy brows. We must've looked like a couple of mindless retirees with nothing better to do than chase a small white ball from manicured green to green.

Like everyone else on the course.

Between bogeys, the client talked. He liked an audience, even if it was paid. His body was thin, but he'd recovered his tan and his agility was unmarred by his recent brush-up with death. The man had a lot more energy than I did.

He liked to yammer between holes. He didn't expect me to say much, so I didn't. That day he kept talking about the everyman, apparently a target of his considerable bile.

Between holes begging for relief from mulligans, he suddenly asked me, "How about your old man, Seymour? Was he an every-day asshole?"

Mr Lasker did not know much about me. He hadn't asked, I hadn't volunteered. No longer a professional griever, I'd become more of a personal assistant. A foil or sidekick. I was a good listener. He seemed to appreciate that about me. And me, I didn't know how to move on.

So the question about my father surprised me. I had to laugh at his undisguised elitism. Nothing phony about Mr Lasker, he was proud to be a bigot and a snob.

We were sitting side by side in the crisp electric cart, heading for the eighteenth hole. I said, "My father was a history professor at a low caliber night school. Most of his students were pre-law men, with the occasional bright woman. I guess you could say he was an all-around asshole when he left us for one of his students." With my pocket handkerchief, I wiped the sweat from my forehead. Some had dripped in my eyes and was smarting. "My mother never got past the betrayal. Guess I was on her side, because I didn't bother to track him down after he took off with the girl."

Mr Lasker shook his head. He was a small man with an oversize head and a lion's mane of gray hair. "Most men are emotional retards with poor impulse control. I mean no disrespect to your dad, Seymour. Men of our fathers' generation, they had massive character armor. Massive, and with no way to open that up. Except in the company of an adoring woman."

We glided to a stop and the breeze died with the cart. The heat level was registering probable sunstroke. Mr Lasker stepped out of the cart. "Wives are not adoring women, Seymour. As you are well aware."

Was I? Well, yes, I was indeed. But I hadn't told him that.

I ignored the remark, still hung up on his comments regarding my absentee father. "So I'm supposed to forgive him for what he did to us, deserting us like that? Taking off with some bimbo, leaving my mom in a rundown apartment with a ten-year-old and no financial support?"

Mr Lasker reached for his golf bag. "You mean, do you forgive the choice he made? Or do you instead continue to be angry at the rest of the world? Do you keep on hating all the well-adjusted families who live like they're in some stupid fucking sitcom? Yeah, I'd say you've spent enough time wallowing in your infantile rage, Seymour. Face the fucking facts: your father was an everyday ass-hole. There's millions of them out there, trying to make life work for themselves. Like you, hanging around here in this oasis of tropical perfection you despise, whiling away your days playing babysitter with me."

I sat there in shock. He'd never spoken to me like that before. Our conversations were all healing nurture, the meaning of life, and poetic philosophy. Wow. He must've been feeling much better.

More like his old self, perhaps.

He walked off, heading steadily toward the tee. His stride was quick and sure. The man was fit.

All day I'd been wondering if Mr Lasker had Raymond on retainer or whether I constituted a one-time fee. I didn't feel it was right to ask, mainly because my host had been treating me so well. But if Raymond was making money off my ongoing babysitting services, I deserved a cut.

On the way to return the golf cart, I told Mr Lasker I would be leaving in the morning. The job was done.

Instantly, the man's attitude changed. "Forgive me for trying to prod you toward introspection, my friend. You are a valued person here. You saved my life, Seymour," he said in a soft voice. "You brought me back from the brink of self-induced obliteration, of letting go of my life too soon. You reminded me how much I care about living. You are important to me. Why can't you stay on indefinitely? Don't I take care of your needs? What's there for you to go home to anyway?"

Not much.

I shrugged. After all, he *was* taking care of my needs. Nice private pool house apartment. Good food. Exercise. Regular outings in my fancy new wardrobe.

But this wasn't real. And my real life still existed, back in Emerald Day Village. I had bills to pay. A job. And I needed to go back to work. I wanted, I realized, to go back to work.

I said, "I have a pet cat. Catcher. He's a stray, but I feed him." This sounded weak. "I have a girlfriend, too," I lied. Marnie was no longer my girlfriend. She wasn't anybody's girlfriend anymore. "She's more of a casual girl I see now and then, casually," I stuttered lamely. "But I've been up here a pretty long time. And, well, you know."

I wasn't lying about that. It had been a very long time since I'd gotten any.

His face lit up. With interest? Happiness for me? Lust? "Go ahead and invite her up for a few days. I'd be happy to entertain your lady friend, Seymour."

I wondered exactly what he meant by entertain. He'd admitted he didn't have the cleanest record with his own women. His wives hadn't lasted very long. He had a sort of pump and dump approach to matrimony. For example, his unfaithful first wife had left him under what he called "mysterious circumstances." According to Mr Lasker, the "ungrateful bitch" suddenly stopped spending her weekends in the Hamptons. I wondered if she'd ever been seen *anywhere* since they'd split up. There were questions regarding the whereabouts of a more recent wife, too, a young woman Mr Lasker had divorced the year before his prognosis sent him into a tailspin. He'd referred to her as "permanently dumped."

He sure didn't have any female visitors on his premature death bed. In fact, no one had come by. Unless they were employed to be there. Lawn maintenance. Cleaning lady. Chef. Reiki master. Bodyguard. Me. It seemed strange. He was obviously connected. A mobster type. And he was rich, with the splendid ego of a retired alpha dog. So shouldn't he have been surrounded by adoring or at least groveling minions? Like the Godfather? Or Tony Soprano?

"I don't think you really want guests right now, Mr Lasker. You're still recovering." I got out of the cart, grabbed his clubs.

"I'm not a narcissist," Mr Lasker replied, before he headed for the pro shop. "It's just that other people don't interest me much."

I wished that included me. But for some reason, it did not. Fourth Rule of Professional Grievers: We must make perfect our will. I was supposed to be on the job. I was there to help Mr Lasker face death, not run from it.

Despite his lousy score, Mr Lasker was in a bountiful mood. He sat beside me humming while I drove us back to his place.

I was as gloomy as ever.

After I dropped Mr Lasker under the front portico, I pulled his car into the northernmost slot in the four-car garage. My Toyota was parked outside, rust spots sparkling in the sinking sun.

I shut the garage door by remote and wandered around back to sit in the shaded grotto by the pool. Vigo, Mr Lasker's bodyguard and gofer, had the afternoon off. He was probably inside, working out in the suite Mr Lasker provided for him to live in.

Vigo creeped me out. I didn't miss seeing his massive silent bulk looming about. The lout was built like a linebacker. He did not speak and he never met your eyes. Vigo wore a navy silk yarmulke but I was pretty sure he'd been raised Catholic. He couldn't help crossing himself now and again, which is not a good Jewish boy's habit.

I knew such things because I'd been raised Catholic. My father was Jewish. I'd had the best of both worlds.

Sunset was letting the hot air out of the sky. I got down on the Chicago brick pool deck and did five pushups. Just for the hell of it. Then I collapsed on a cream-colored chaise longue. My loafers were slightly damp from the fairways, so I kicked them off. I watched the sky darken as the fiery sun slid down into its hole in the ground behind me.

My eyes felt fat, heavy. Hope was for kids. Why did Mr Lasker want it so much? What would he do with it besides toy with it here on his private playground? And what good was playing around with hope all by yourself? Why had I even offered it to him? Now I was hopelessly stuck.

I must have dozed off because when I opened my eyes, Mr Lasker was dragging a turquoise sling chair in my direction. He sat down and immediately lit up a skinny joint. "Medical marijuana," he explained.

I didn't comment. The man could do whatever he wished.

He propped his horny feet on the drink table between us and coughed lightly. "Let me tell you a little story, Seymour."

Mr Lasker was not much of a storyteller but he sure liked to talk. I'd already heard about the "bullshit" IRS raids on his New York publishing business that preceded the retirement/flight to Boca. This was how he'd described his business code of ethics: "Take what you like, pay nobody, sell in bulk." His company was well respected, he said, for the cutting-edge financial and business trade books, macroeconomics texts, and corporate newsletters he'd specialized in for decades. Mr Lasker seemed proud of his "seedy investors." He didn't go into detail, though. Not with me. Like his tales about the women in his life, Mr Lasker provided only the rough outline, letting me fill in the rest myself. His mythic yet oddly non-narrative stories usually ended with the claim, "I've spent my life divesting myself of undesirable assets."

The quick and easy way he wiped clean the slate of his life!

Still, he sketched himself as the humble but savvy businessman from Queens who was trying to make the best of things in South Florida. I knew what he meant, though, when he said, "They fuck you night and day in this place." Florida is an alien tropical world that best suits reptilian brains designed to accept the swamp sludge of a life spent dawdling in wet heat. It can be difficult for a civilized man to make sense of his life here.

Mr Lasker exhaled a plume of greenish smoke. "First, some hard-earned words of advice, Seymour. Don't go crawling back to your girlfriend unless she's worth it." He frowned at me. "Women, they make a man feel small enough, he can disappear from his own view. I loved a fabulous woman once, Seymour. She became everything to me, provided all my heat and light. Then I let her take me down, way down to that fucking cold dark place. You know what I mean when I say that fucking cold dark place?"

I nodded. What red-blooded male didn't?

He turned away and coughed hard into his crooked elbow, then snuffed the joint between two fingers. He carefully placed it in a breast pocket of his candy-cane striped robe. "Even speaking about her makes me feel sick inside. This woman, she was ambrosia. Honey poured on your skin slowly, slowly. She was cool and smooth and sweet and delicious. You are loving it so much you fail to notice you're stripped naked and staked in the sand, lying spread-eagled in the desert sun. You go to sit up and you find you can't move. You start to itch and then you're on fire. Then you see you're covered with fucking ants. And flies, big huge spiders. Fucking scorpions."

He shook his big shaggy head. "Sad thing. She turned out to be just another pain in the ass asset that hadda be divested. Just like always."

I was still waiting for the story when Mr Lasker jumped up, stretching. His torso was trim, tight, like a marathon runner. He looked good. Better than me and he was the one with the lethal disease.

27

He went over to the chickee hut and stepped behind the bar. I sat on the edge of my deck chair, sniffing the warm sweet air. Gardenias and the night jasmine hedge by the veranda were in bloom. The cicadas called out to one another in an insect version of the dating yodel.

Mr Lasker had his back to me, but I could smell the gin when it splashed onto the ice cubes. I smelled the lime when he sliced through its hard green skin. My hands trembled and my eyes began to water. I hadn't had a drop of alcohol since pulling myself out of my own deathbed, which was six months after the last time I saw Marnie. Which was after twenty-four solid weeks of black hole drinking, firewater straight out of the bottle, enough rotgut booze to blow up my liver enzymes and put me in the hospital for another month of blackness.

But not nearly enough to destroy my memories.

When Mr Lasker turned around, he had two glasses, one in each gnarled hand.

Shit. Was I strong enough to say no to this man? To myself?

As if reading my mind, he handed me the glass and said, "Tonight we drink, Seymour. But only tonight."

You didn't say no to Mr Lasker. So I thanked him with a curt nod, and lifted the glass to my lips. The pine smell tickled my nose and the bubbles went down easy. They went down so fucking easy.

"This hack I hired to write my biography? Guy said something to me once, Seymour. Something I never forgot. Man was a celebrity ghostwriter, a real dummy, but he had a fucking bead on it, he really did."

Mr Lasker pointed to the blue-black night sky. The stars were out in droves. He quoted the biographer in a high and mighty voice, like one of those spoken-word poets so full of their own linguistic superiority. "Happiness is a taste that lingers in the mind, not on the tongue, so you must keep going back for more."

True. And I felt happiness in that fleeting moment. I allowed my body to melt into the deck chair. Everything slipped away and I was glad it was all gone.

When Mr Lasker placed his drink on the table beside me I eyed it greedily. Then I finished up my own.

"Seymour, Seymour, Seymour," he intoned dreamily. His glass beckoned to me, so I set mine on the table beside it. "I'm giving you an opportunity here. To move beyond your own darkness, beyond that cold dark place. You see? Forget about her, Seymour. Women like that? They bring men like us too fucking close to death."

This was true also. I thought about telling him about Marnie, I was feeling that loose. He seemed to know anyway. But I said nothing, my mind drifting pleasantly.

Mr Lasker's cell phone rang. He pulled it out of the side pocket of his dressing gown. "Speak," he said to the caller.

The voice on the other end was a distant rumble. Mr Lasker turned his back and said, "So you say."

As soon as he stood up and walked away, I reached for his drink. I held his glass to my lips. I could taste the happiness, the forgetfulness on my tongue. I took a greedy gulp, then returned Mr Lasker's drink to the table. He still had his back to me.

"And what can I do to thank you for your call?" he said, after turning in my direction. His eyes skated over me, and he turned away again.

I picked up his drink again. I savored the gin and put up with the tonic, ashamed of my inherent weakness and amazed by the power of the everyman asshole's thirst for self-destruction.

I drink, therefore I am.

Useless.

Weak.

A loser.

Apparently, my prior tolerance for liquor had dropped significantly during my dry spell. By the time Mr Lasker slid the phone back in his pocket, I was already delightfully drunk. I molded myself to the chair, enveloped in the gentle warmth of the night, staring up at the pinprick stars.

Suddenly Mr Lasker appeared above me. He looked down at me, an indecipherable expression on his face. His head was like the sun. The sun with a tan. A suntan!

I giggled, then in slow motion reached over to place his empty glass beside my own on the table. Was he mad at me for stealing his drink?

"Your power lies in your pretense of powerlessness, Seymour," he said in a low voice.

Sounded like a new rule. A rule for everyday assholes.

Then my client friend reached down and grabbed me by the throat. His hands were old, all spotted and veiny, but strong enough to close off my air passageways.

My vision blurred and I struggled, but not hard enough.

"Nobody lies to me, especially some snoop bastard," I heard him mutter. His words came from what sounded like a great distance away, his gravelly voice tickling my eardrums from across the still swimming pool, from some invisible point miles out to sea.

I would've defended myself (*snoop bastard*?) but I couldn't speak. I was drunk, choking, about to black out.

The last thing I heard him say was, "You got some stories of your own, you fucking son of a bitch."

I woke up under a prickly bush, flat on my back on the damp grass. I could smell the ocean brine, the waves close enough for me to hear the repetitive scratch of sea on sand. My tongue felt thick and sore and my throat hurt. I couldn't move.

Scared I might be paralyzed, I lay still while my mind panicked. Eventually I felt a buzzy numbness. I jiggled my fingers and toes, gradually reawakening my body's extremities.

As I dragged myself out from under the low-hanging bougainvillea, nasty little thorns scraped my bare skin. My back seized up on me and my legs were rubbery, so I stood up slowly, and very carefully. My head throbbed. I was still wearing my pastel golf shorts, my car keys in the front pocket. My duffel bag, the one I'd brought to Boca with me when I took on the job, sat on the grass a few feet away.

I looked around. Apparently I was in a public park near the beach. I had to assume it was Mr Lasker, aided by the hulking Vigo, who'd dumped me there.

At least I had not been permanently dumped.

My phone started ringing. I crawled around on all fours until I found my cell, tossed in between the high roots of a banyan tree.

I checked the screen. Raymond. What perfect timing!

I tried to answer, not sure my voice would work. It didn't. I croaked.

"Seymour?" Raymond sounded concerned. "Are you all right?"

"I think so." My words were charred, froglike. My balance was off, too, so I dropped down on the cool grass, lay back. "I think Mr Lasker fired me. But first he choked me half to death."

Raymond laughed. "Whoops! You were supposed to help *him* die, not the other way around."

He kept chuckling, like this was a funny story we could tell at parties. I was tempted to hang up, but I was too beaten down to do it.

Adopting a more serious tone, he said, "The job of a professional griever has its inherent risks. After all, those who feel they must resort to staging and staffing their own deaths tend to be unpleasant people. Some have criminal backgrounds. You cannot expect to befriend a person like that. Waste and void, Seymour, waste and void. Please don't be as naïve about your responsibilities next time around."

A blush of heat crawled up my neck. Marnie had called me

naïve, and worse. She'd accused me of being unwilling to contemplate the meaning of meaninglessness. "Only your own life needs you to be there for it to go on," she'd admonished me. More than once.

"Look at it this way," Raymond said. "Our job is to help the suffering in their wrestle with death. We help these people learn how to die and by doing so we learn how to live. If you help them cling to life, Seymour, they won't learn a thing. And neither will you."

He stopped speaking just long enough for me to resign myself to my latest dismal failure. It was a not unfamiliar feeling. I stared at the ominous clouds chasing one another across a navy-blue velvet sky. I closed my eyes and listened to the wind rising off the ocean as it manhandled crisp palm fronds and leafy banyan branches. I could smell the approaching rain. It smelled rich, thick with unknown elements and promises. Like the earth itself.

Raymond cleared his throat. "I see why you might feel you deserve danger pay for this particular case. Perhaps that will make up for losing the second half of your fee and the bonus. You're a good worker and I'd like to keep you happy."

Happy?

This cracked me up. For the first time in a very long while I laughed; only it hurt my poor bruised throat, so I didn't laugh for long.

Long enough, though. Long enough to remember how it felt to feel good.

Coffee Spoons II

M ORE COFFEE SPOONS on the table.

As long as you're interested enough in my story to keep reading, it's only fair that I explain what will be left out. Here's what you won't be hearing about from me: my ex-wife's legal victories that reduced me to a poverty-level income until she finally married the pizza franchise millionaire; my mother's quick mental decline and subsequent degenerative years in a sad series of drab nursing homes; the on-again, off-again love affair I had with the drink, a romantic attachment I'd learned from my father.

I also don't want to tell you about the horrible accidental deaths of three of my childhood dogs: all mutts from the pound with too short lifespans. All the deaths (a suspicious poisoning, not uncommon in our less than desirable neighborhood; a fast-growing tumor on a soft pink belly; and a gory hit-and-run) I mourned loudly and genuinely until the replacement puppy arrived.

Always the replacement puppy, the quick distraction, the new focus to divert the grief.

No wonder I became a master of emotional detours.

Do I have to explain how I came to be an old man sleeping with much younger women? No, I don't want to go into all that here. Besides, it's not so difficult for you to imagine why. If you'd led a similar life, you'd probably be doing exactly what I did. In fact by reading this now you might just be living out your own fantasies, vicariously, through me. I don't judge you for that. Besides, you can easily figure out the subconscious (and conscious) reasons why I go for these lovely girls: the cultural aversion to aging, the contemporary fear of mortality, Madison Avenue and YouTube. The *Sports Illustrated* swimsuit issue. These things have their hold on you, too; so there's no need for me to burden you with your own self-delusions.

Our shared delusions.

About life. Death. Immortality.

That's why I've thinned my story down to the bone. I've cut out the meaty details you don't need to know.

For example: you don't really need to know how I got here because you're at a similar place yourself right now, or you will be soon enough, and you will get there in your own way. On your own blind path, on your own uncontrollable journey. Virus or no virus, we all head down the road to the same inevitable end. No, the details of an individual life don't matter. Not in the end. And the end is closer than we care to think.

Check your rearview mirror: everything behind you is closer than it appears. Much closer. Your life is catching up to you. Fast.

None of these digressions move my story along, do they? Here's the sad ugly truth: much of life is spent in purposeless digression. Birth and death: those are the end-points on a bizarre unknown continuum governed by a dispassionate fate.

Fate, to me, means a lot of waiting around to see what will happen.

Maybe nothing does. Or nothing much. And then it's over. No wonder the funeral parlors are half empty.

That's *your* half.

But there do occur points of what I call critical mass in the average life (and, let's admit it, most lives are average – or sub-average). They happen when the build-up of small insignificant details reaches a kind of pressure-cooker peak; and then, suddenly, surprising things happen. Ideas come to fruition. Perceptions shift, new and exciting paradigms arise. You see yourself more clearly, and you look like someone completely different than you were, than you'd always been. Where are you really coming from? And what is it you really want?

Critical mass can bring great happiness. And it can bring over-whelming grief. Usually both. But we ignore the grief. Tuck it away for later. Sweep it under the hotel bed for someone else to clean up.

Eventually, all that unexplored unacknowledged grief achieves a critical mass of its own. That's when we have the opportunity to take stock. Some people do, some don't. I didn't, not for a long time. But eventually, I would be forced by fate to do so. It makes a good story.

Once my story has been told, you may choose to focus on your own. Before your particular inscrutable fate steps in and steals the opportunity away from you.

A Game of Chess

AFTER THE CONVERSATION with Raymond I picked myself up off the park grass and drove home. The sky vibrated with pale blue early morning clarity and as the sun rose the palm trees radiated a vivid green. The air felt light and it tasted sweet. My body ached, I could hardly swallow my throat was so painful, but all I could think was this: I'm alive, I'm *alive, I am alive.*

My home welcomed me with its humble sameness. Without changing or unpacking, I fell on my bed and let sleep overtake me.

The landline on the night table beside my bed rang. I answered it, then hung up without speaking. The room was bright, I hadn't drawn the shades, but I couldn't make myself wake up. So I lay there and drifted in and out of sleep until the phone started in again.

Each time I awoke, I realized I was still alive, but somehow less alive than before.

Sometime later I found myself sitting on the edge of the bed with the phone receiver in my hand. Had I been speaking to someone? I listened, then said hello.

"Are you awake this time?" Raymond. He said, "I'll call back again in an hour if you're still asleep."

"I'm coming to," I admitted. "Although I'd rather not."

I'd been in a dream with a green mountain, and birds, sea birds: like terns only much larger. Big black birds. A barreling truck, and lots of rolling oranges, Florida oranges. Marnie was there, and she was pregnant, her red dress billowing like a gown, her belly wonderfully huge. The tone was romantic drama with unspoken tragic undertones. I held the images in my mind, trying to imbue them with meaning.

Raymond kept talking and the images faded.

"So, I have another job lined up for you, a short-term gig this time. Come by the office today and I'll fill you in. And I'll pay you for the Lasker job. A kill fee, we'll call it."

He laughed.

I didn't. My good mood had dried up like a gin and tonic left out in the Florida sun. My neck hurt: I could feel the imprint of Mr Lasker's bony fingers around the base of my throat.

I lashed out at my employer. "Did he tell you *why* he frigging choked me until I passed out? Did your upscale Boca client explain why he suddenly unloaded me like a sack of *garbage*? Why he left me lying in a heap, unconscious, alone in a park like some stinking wino? Hey, he could've killed me, Raymond. Or I could've gotten mugged, rolled, roughed up. I was out cold, lying there half the night. I might have gotten arrested for malingering."

My anger made me feel less grateful that I was alive, more upset that I almost wasn't.

"Mr Lasker is not the most cooperative client, true," Raymond agreed in an unctuous voice that immediately increased my ire. "But you're fine, aren't you? Home safe and all that? And about to get paid! With more work waiting for you!"

Raymond was such a phony prick. He'd grasped my bare bones financial situation, so he knew how easy it was to manipulate me. I wondered what else he knew about me.

"So, Raymond, what exactly did you say to Mr Lasker yesterday?" I was guessing the call just prior to the attack came from Raymond: the phone call that had turned my generous client friend into a homicidal maniac. Could Raymond have precipitated the sudden transformation? "What did you tell him about me? What did you say that made him decide to dump me like that?"

Raymond was silent. He knew that I knew it was him, and that was enough to convict him.

After a long minute, however, he sighed. "Well, I guess I told him your mother was an Irish Catholic."

I snorted. "So? So I'm not *Jewish*? That the kind of information which can drive men like Mr Lasker into a murderous rage?"

I flashed on Vigo and his secretive signs of the cross. Could it have been that simple?

No. This was bullshit. Mr Lasker didn't care about my heritage, my religious choices. I knew the man better than that. Yet here was Raymond, admitting he made the call that so painfully ended my little vacation among the upper crust. But for what? So I could go back to work for him? Go sit in a half-empty pew at some loner's upcoming funeral mass? What was Raymond's motivation? He'd been so adamant that I needed to stay and finish the job.

Raymond cleared his throat. "I also might've mentioned you're retired. From twenty-five years as, well, an IRS auditor." He paused, then laughed nervously. "I guess he jumped to conclusions."

I stood up, accidently yanking the phone off the nightstand. It crashed to the floor, but I held on to the receiver. "Oh, he jumped all right. He jumped on my chest and wrapped his manicured paws around my freaking windpipe. Jesus, Raymond. Why the hell did you tell him *that*?"

Actually, I wasn't nearly as disturbed by this news as I should've been. Maybe because I wasn't clear why a lie like that would get me choked and ditched. I was physically exhausted after what I'd been through, and this must have made me dense. Because I didn't get it.

I said, "This your idea of a practical joke?"

Raymond spluttered. "I was trying to get you out of there. You were absolutely haunting me with all your whine and complain calls. You'd been hanging around Boca Raton for weeks. I thought I'd help out, but I had to be subtle about it. Remember, Mr Lasker is a paying client and he will come back to us. So I . . . I invented a backstory for you." He paused, calmed. "The elite hate the IRS. This was a way to get you relieved of your duties. I never meant for you to get hurt."

Elite, my skinny ass. Mafioso was more like it. I seethed in silence.

He cajoled. "Seymour, I want to make it up to you. This kind of thing, well, it never happens to my employees. I'm so very sorry. I feel responsible. Please come in and pick up your pay. I won't be able to relax until I know you have been paid generously for your trouble."

What I was thinking was how I could use a drink, but I had no alcohol in the house. I'd stripped my place of booze when I went on the wagon. Now I wanted off. I could use my pay to buy that drink for myself. To stock up again, replenish my empty home bar. I was owed. Owed big time.

I sighed loudly and dramatically. "Fine. I'll come by in an hour or so, and you can tell me where the hell you get off putting my life in danger like that. Right now I need to eat something and feed the cat." I was speaking more to myself than to my employer.

He started to respond, but before he could carry on trying to placate me I disconnected. Then I unplugged the phone and left it on the floor.

The shower offered comfort, the steam loosening my sore muscles. My neck felt bruised, tender to the touch. I was still confused about the furious attack on me. Okay, so I wasn't Jewish. My grandfather was Jewish and I got his name. So what? I'd never told Mr Lasker I was a Jew. Maybe the poetry misled him? If so, I hadn't done it on purpose. I love the Jewish poets. They know how to dampen the mood in a way that makes you feel better about your own neuroses. Like Woody Allen in his films.

Toweling dry, I pledged that I would not apologize for my taste in art. Mr Lasker couldn't give a shit about that. More likely Mr Lasker was a tax delinquent, worried I was there to spy on his finances, ultra-paranoid about years of laundering and skimming off the top. Those concerns were the kind I could understand. But his attack on me was misguided. Such a waste. Because I'd never worked for the US government in the revenue department – or in any capacity. I was weak at math: my worst subject. All Mr Lasker had to do was undertake a background check to discover how I'd retired from the Boston public school system after decades of thankless duty in decrepit classrooms, teaching English.

Dressed in a pair of cheap shorts and a white tee shirt, I stepped out on the patio. The humidity dropped on me like a damp blanket. Ugh.

Catcher was a tight circle of fur on the moldy wicker chair. I was carrying an open can of tuna, so he lifted his little head and stared, whiskers twitching.

He wasn't my cat, but he might as well have been.

The patio had been screened in once, but Hurricane Wilma ripped it all out. Without screening to block his path, Catcher was able to come and go as he pleased. He'd adopted me for this reason. And for the tuna handouts.

Meowing loudly, he sprang down, heading for the corner where I usually set his food. I served him at once. Catcher was the perfect companion. He never scolded or gave me the furry eyeball when dinner was late. This time it was weeks late, but the cat just rolled with it. No snide comments, no complaints.

I stood there in the afternoon heat and watched him eat. He was so delicate in his bites, so well-mannered. He must've been someone's pet once, a pampered domestic at some point in his life. Before being abandoned by the people who pretended to love him.

He busied himself licking out all the tiny flakes still sticking to the can. The wind had picked up and I could smell approaching rain. When an overgrown cabbage palm scratched against the tile roof, Catcher looked up, momentarily distracted. He switched his long black tail, then returned to the tuna flakes.

I bent down and stroked his bony back.

Later, Catcher would rub himself against my legs and purr contentedly. In the meantime, I needed coffee.

On my way to the office to pick up my pay I got stuck in the traffic slugging along Federal Highway. My air conditioner was broken, so I had the windows open. I was therefore inhaling exhaust fumes tempered with the fast food grease oozing out of the pizza and burger joints I was crawling past. The endless stretch of pawn shops, drive-throughs, and down-at-the-heels liquor stores made me miss ultra-clean Boca Raton. But only for a minute. That city was a nest of vipers, con-men and their plastic surgery wives. Mobsters and murderers.

Waste and void, waste and void, I reminded myself.

I adjusted the sun visor and started thinking about my role as a professional griever. What if people saw me as a kind of vulture? What if they realized that whenever I was hanging around someone had recently died? These questions disturbed me, but I deliberately put them out of my mind when I turned into the parking-lot of Raymond's office.

Professional Grievers, Inc., was located in a rundown strip mall. I parked in front of Sexxxy Nail Bait, ostensibly a manicurist's shop, and took the dirty cement stairs up to the second floor, where a row of windowless offices faced north. I entered the nondescript door behind which Raymond ran his business.

The receptionist's desk was empty, just like it was whenever I came by. Did Raymond have a receptionist? I had never seen one.

"Seymour!" Raymond rushed down the hall, grinning like the guilty phony he was. "You look good. Tanned and fit. And no visible signs of wear and tear from your night under the stars," he said with a wry smile. "Even the homeless bums in Boca live better than most of us working hacks. Right?"

I grimaced. "I hope this isn't your way of saying you're sending me back there on another job?"

He said it wasn't, not to worry, and I followed him down the short hall to his dark office. The single window was shuttered with an old hurricane awning that kept out both light and heat. The room was cold. I sank into the green faux-leather club chair by his desk and tilted back my head. Raymond groaned dramatically when he saw the bruises on my throat.

I said in a mean voice, "Was that the best job you could find for me? What, only the rich assholes are dying these days? No paying customers among the little people? No virus deaths lacking mourners? People with no history of brutality?"

He sat down on the matching leather seat beside me. "I am *so* sorry about what happened with Mr Lasker. He did call this morning to tell me I was a hundred percent wrong about your work history. He said to have you call him, he'd like to speak with you."

Fat chance.

I stared at him, stony and silent.

Raymond stood up, moving to his huge oak desk and perching on the edge of it. Sympathy time had ended. I could see him taking up the position of authority now, literally as well as figuratively looking down on me.

The surface of his desk was as clean as a cutting board. No family photos cluttered his desktop. Except for basic furniture, the office was bare. No framed diplomas relieved the emptiness of the pale yellow walls: nothing to indicate what kind of business operated there, or what kind of person operated it.

Before he could launch into his latest pitch, I said, "No gigs today. I don't feel like talking to anyone right now."

I was about to demand my money when he reached back and slid a business envelope across his desk. He picked it up and handed it to me.

"Except for maybe you, Raymond," I said, peeking inside the white envelope at the thick stack of hundred-dollar bills.

"Understandable." When he crossed his legs, I checked out his shoes. Capezios, mirror shined. "But you might just give Mr Lasker a call back, Seymour. No need to anger the man. He's still a client."

This pissed me off. I began to steam in the cold dark room. What nerve this guy had to tell *me* what to do, to warn me to make nice with the homicidal maniac who'd *strangled me until I blacked out*.

But as soon as I looked at Raymond's face, I knew I had to let it go. Raymond's grey eyes were icy, as distant and foreboding as the Arctic. Winter in Greenland. I clasped the envelope of money to my chest and looked away, waiting for my blood pressure to return to normal.

Calmly he said, "I believe Mr Lasker wishes to apologize to you for the misunderstanding. No harm in that. He won't ask you to return to Boca, not right now. I've informed him you're about to embark on another grief case for me."

Raymond smoothed his hand-painted tie. The marigolds on the tie were so bright his fingers looked yellow when he ran them across the silk.

"The next case is an easy one, Seymour. A formal Irish wake, the high mass followed by a lakeside ceremony with the ashes. They need attendance at the wake and mass, the lake is optional. Think you're up for that?"

I didn't. Not yet. Maybe in a few days. After I'd restocked my liquor cabinet and revisited my passion for the drink.

Seeing my hesitation, Raymond added, "This is a two-day assignment, and I'm willing to pay eight hundred. Up front."

He reached inside his jacket to remove his billfold. I admired the smooth leather, the kind of long wallet specially designed to slide gracefully in and out of an expensive suit jacket.

The guy had cash tucked in all kinds of places.

He counted out the payment on his big bare desk. Not even a blotter. What kind of company was this anyway? No other employees around, no sign on the front door, no checks with taxes deducted.

And plenty of crisp-looking bills.

Raymond handed me the money. Then he said, "In pre-industrial societies, death was accepted as an inevitable aspect of everyday life. Grieving for the recently deceased in our pre-tech society was equated with simplicity, meaningful ceremony, and acceptance of what was widely regarded as a public experience. Death in those days was highly visible, allowing everyone to stand in its shadow and survive, to look it in the face and walk on. Or not. The power of death had widespread respect. Death was held in high regard. Death held such sway over the public imagination it was depicted in much of the literature, art, music, and theatre. Death lived, it was here among us, in us and around us. Death made a statement to one's self and others, it was a personal and a communal act."

He straightened his wrinkle-free tie and removed his glasses to rub his nose. He appeared absolutely calm, hands and voice steady, confident. For whom did he dress in all that Armani? Certainly not to impress old slobs like me.

He went on. "But nowadays, dying is a dirty thing. A shameful process. Americans think it's unnecessary! The act of dying has become so technologized and medicalized, it's been depleted of all inherent value. Today, success lies in cheating old age and death, paying for them to go away, overpowering the end of life to trick it into submission. In contemporary society, failure is the inability to outsmart one's own death."

He buffed his glasses lightly with his thousand-dollar tie.

I said nothing.

"Death today is a hidden demon, to be feared and avoided at all costs. When death is confronted, it is usually with shame and without support. Grieving occurs in isolation, the dying hidden away, the mourners ignored. And now there's this virus: it makes us flee one another's company, both before death and afterward. This denial of the reality of death as ultimately human is a failure to accept ourselves as finite living beings."

Raymond stared at me. His empathetic words did not match the cold metallic sheen of his faraway eyes.

I said, "Dying doesn't line up, Raymond. Not with the global imperative to amass money and status. Dying is a sign of weakness nobody wants to think about. Oh, death was okay back in the days when organized religions dominated cultures. Modern-day religions are all about being seen to take part. Getting old and sick, dying slowly and painfully, succumbing to a pandemic, things like this clash with the larger narcissistic agenda."

For some reason, half-remembered lines from a poem by Louise Glück popped into my head: we don't even know what we feel until we hear the word *grief*. I had fallen for Glück many years before. She seemed to know how to express what we may be capable of feeling.

Some of us.

To Raymond I said, "The Irish are still capable of throwing a decent wake, though. So what if they all get shitfaced? At least you can feel things stirring at an Irish funeral."

To my surprise, Raymond laughed. He leaned forward to clasp me on the shoulder. His grip was strong. I felt like I couldn't move until he let go, so I sat there until he did.

I stood up with my bulging envelope, casually placing the nice fat wad in the deep side pocket of my shorts. The envelope pulled me off balance, it was that heavy.

Raymond said, "Seymour, I like you. I like a man who speaks

from experience. This particular Irish death will be a new experience for you. Then you can use this experience in the future. Do
you understand what I am saying?"

I did and I didn't. Either way, money is often able to provide
one with the motivation necessary to put up with bullshit, with
everyday assholes, with getting pushed around and manipulated.
First Rule of Professional Grievers, modified: We create our bank
account from one moment to the next.

I moved toward the door. Over my shoulder, I said, "Raymond, you can give me the details I'll need to do the job. But
you'd better leave what goes on in my head up to me."

Raymond laughed again.

Man of mystery. I would never know what made the guy tick.

Just before I stepped into the hall, he told me to hold on. Then
he leaned over the desk to write down the address of the funeral
home, the church, and the lake where the ashes would be spread.

Proper Fools

S EATED UNOBTRUSIVELY IN a back pew, I fantasized about Marnie. The way her lips felt on mine, the heat of her smooth, almond-scented skin. Then I clicked off the mental video and fell into the blackness, the hole her loss left in my heart. In my life.

I repeated the process for ten minutes or so, working hard to encourage the familiar emotions to well up. I was here to grieve, I needed that old grief to flood over me.

But nothing happened. No tears, no pain in my heart. Just a blank numbness. And a hammering headache.

The chapel in the funeral home was dank and moldy and smelled like wet carnations and lilies. It reminded me of my days as an altar boy at drafty, decrepit St. Joan of Arc. In the winter my hands would be blue by the end of the first mass. Sometimes in the summer I got nauseous from the heat, the incense and flowers. The priests were tough with us but none of them ever touched me. That kind of stuff made me sick to hear. Still, I kept going to mass, kept assisting.

A young fool. But I had hope back then. So much hope.

A woman in a lacy black veil and matching mask seated herself at the far end of my pew. Then she knelt for a few seconds before reseating herself. Dressed expensively, she looked good from my end of the row. She had what I judged to be an excellent ass.

My nascent tears dried themselves off and slid back down their ducts.

Grieving wasn't happening the way it usually did. I was too distracted. The woman in my pew, the time spent with Mr Lasker, all the money Raymond was paying me to do this stuff and I couldn't even do it properly. My mind flitted ticishly. I tried to capture it, hold it down, make it think that it was Marnie in the big silver urn on the altar.

All my efforts failed.

When the woman in my row shifted, I inhaled a drifting scent of fruity perfume. She smelled too delicious for a funeral.

The priest appeared before the altar and stood facing the sparse audience in the chapel. In a booming papal baritone he began to speak, and the woman in my pew slid along until she was seated right next to me. Her face and hair were obscured by the chin-length netted veil and oversize mask, but her legs were visible. Long and lovely, like the thin hands she folded so demurely in her narrow lap. Her physical features reminded me of Marnie. I wanted to bend down and let her scratch my head with her squared-off nails.

"Blah, blah, blah," blathered the priest.

There was no way I would be able to shed a single tear. I couldn't listen to his clichéd sermon, and I was unable to resurrect my own sadness for the benefit of the people around me. For all I knew, they were as emotionally uninvolved as I was, sitting there daydreaming while he sermonized.

I was wondering whether the woman beside me might be one of Raymond's employees when she leaned close. "He's so full of shit," she whispered.

I recognized the voice, the slight Boston lilt.

Yvonne, the woman from the wake I'd attended the day before. A wake held for the man in the urn up on the altar.

My stomach heaved a bit and I felt woozy. Maybe I shouldn't have had that glass of wine at four a.m.

Glass? Try tumbler. Try fishbowl, try *aquarium.*

The thing was, I couldn't sleep. Neither could Catcher. So we sat out on the patio while I indulged. The humid air wet my skin and fogged up the wine bottle. Catcher left paw prints on the cement floor.

My head was still damp and foggy. Something sinister in my skull throbbed and a tiny prick of light pierced my brain like a laser. Now that I had pocket money and sporadic employment, the wagon I'd once been so determined not to fall off had receded into the distance without me. Bye-bye wagon.

My home bar was fully restocked.

The previous evening's wake had led me to indulge in a binge. Or so I told myself. I really had no excuse. Drink had gotten me into trouble all my life. It would surely do so again.

The Irish know how to party. They also know how to host a mournful event, something I had observed too many times during my childhood. In Boston I wasn't the only kid with carrot hair, masses of freckles (*a tan through a screen*, they called it), and a sunburn starting every fourth of July. There were plenty of Clearys and Callahans, Mahers and O'Briens in my neighborhood. And when one of them died, we all packed into Shea Brothers Funeral Home, then walked across the parking lot to St. Joan of Arc for the mass. For the few days before and a few days after, the party at the home of the bereaved was continuous. Liquor flowing, bawdy jokes and family stories, plate after plate of cold cuts and the kind of cakes and pastries our moms usually refused to purchase. A lot of laughing and running around. Weddings were similar, another good reason for everyone to drink and gab, flirt and gossip, drink and drink some more.

The wake for the new client, a successful middle-aged businessman named Bill Manahan, was something else. It was held in a gothic funeral parlor a few miles into the Everglades. A handful of unmasked people were milling around the chilly fluorescent-lit room when I arrived sometime after eight. I removed my own mask, tucked it in my jacket pocket.

The guest book had dozens of signatures in it. I created a scrawl with my left hand, then scrawled again where the ledger requested a printed version of each guest's name. Better not to leave a paper trail. Patriot Act and all that. I was wary now. Who knew what the deceased had been up to? Why get involved any more than I had to?

The gold chalice that held the man's ashes was displayed on a high, lace-covered table at the front of the viewing room. Surrounding the urn, a photo montage depicted Mr Manahan at various memorable points in his life. I padded across the ultra-thick carpeting and hung around the bulletin boards, examining them for clues to what I might say should anyone ask how I knew the departed. If no one asked me anything, I would offer little in the way of communication.

Raymond had advised me not to make a scene.

Me, make a scene? Hardly likely, not at my age.

The corkboard I chose to peruse first held a grainy, scalloped-edged shot of a squinting boy on a red Schwinn bicycle. Then there was a yellowed Polaroid of a young man in a royal blue graduation gown. Several professional wedding photos, the bride heavily made up and model thin in her Victorian gown, the groom red-faced and proud in a bizarre white tux. A clipping from a Boston State College alumni magazine listed Bill's name under *Golden Angel Donors*.

Go, Bill.

I might have been at BSC when Bill matriculated. I wasn't, but I might have been.

Good enough.

I walked past the urn, not sure whether to stop and bow my head or kneel down before it or what. Exactly what was cremation urn protocol?

I made my way over to a young man in a black Zegna suit,

standing alone in the back of the room. The guy was built like a weightlifter and he stared blankly, leaning heavily against a faux Greek pillar. His tight jacket stretched across his wide shoulders, and his hands were rounded and huge, like punching bags on his wrists.

"I would like to offer my condolences to the widow. Can you point her out to me? Mr Manahan is . . . *was* an old friend from Boston," I explained. My brow had wet itself so I mopped the cold sweat with my handkerchief and waited for a response.

None was forthcoming. The man responded instead to the ring of his cell phone. He turned his back on me and rushed out of the room, phone to his ear.

So much for a party atmosphere at *this* Irish wake.

An elderly woman in a timeless Chanel suit caught my eye. She sat alone on a smooth wooden bench directly under the exit sign. Her hair was that pinkish color not found in nature, but her green eyes sparkled and she actually smiled up at me as I approached.

"May I join you?" I whispered. She patted the seat beside her, so I sat down a few feet away. "Quite a turnout," I said.

Sweat dripped down my chest on to the crest of my stomach and pooled there. My sport coat was a holdover from my Boston days and much too heavy for South Florida, but I'd be damned if I'd spend any of my pay on costuming. Cheaper and easier to keep playing the role of shy loser friend from the old days. The down and out friend nobody talked about. You know the type. No need for me to dress up for that part.

"All the big bosses already came and went," she said to me in the proper hushed tones used in this type of room. "The big men from New York and Philly. All of them came to pay their respects." She sounded proud, full of brag. I wondered if Mr Manahan was her son or if she might be, like me, a paid mourner. "Which family are you with?" she asked me, reaching up to adjust her black pillbox hat. It looked like an original, a relic from the days of Jackie Kennedy.

"Is the widow present?" I asked.

My eyes were on the three women in short black dresses and stranded pearls huddling in a far corner. I was guessing one of these *uber*-thin women was the widow. Maybe the widow and her daughters? My plan was to approach the family, pay my respects, and leave. This time out I wanted to complete the work assigned with no extenuating circumstances.

"Of course she is," the little lady admonished me. She was shrunken and couldn't have weighed a hundred pounds. Still, I hesitated to piss her off. There was something akin to the Mother Superior about her. "You must be with the other side," she said, and frowned. Then she looked me up and down. "You weren't at the house, I'd remember you. Who're you with?"

Couldn't I just be a distant friend paying my respects? Why the skeptical inquisition? "Old college friend of Bill's," I said, and started to stand up. Time to move things along. My new liquor cache was calling to me.

She clasped my wrist and squeezed, pincer-like. I remained half-seated, my ass a few inches above the bench.

"How nice. Bill had so many old friends. You should come back to the house. Quite a few of Bill's old friends will be there."

Her hands felt more claw than flesh. She seemed unwilling to let me go.

I said, "Thank you. I'll try to do that."

I was hoping this answer would win me my freedom. My wrist hurt: a few fingers were going numb.

But she only squeezed tighter. "Do you know the Berry brothers? They'll be there, at the house. They came in last night from Jersey."

When I shook my head – no, I didn't know the Berry

brothers — she dropped my hand like it was infectious. She rose much too quickly for a frail old lady and marched away.

The piped-in muzak at funeral home wakes is always a mix of WASPy church hymns and dumbed down classical songs, the kind of moronic melodies that can slip inside your brain and replay in your mind for days. It's usually the most intolerable aspect of attending such events. As I sat back down on the wafer-thin pillow on the bench, I watched the nimble crone march to a watery version of Beethoven's "Ode to Joy," ruining forever for me that beautiful song. I was about to turn away, to try to erase the image of the angry biddy in black, when she made her approach for landing on the three young women.

None of them looked pleased when she crashed their huddle.

One by one, the three young women turned to look at me, their faces lovely, pale, with large eyes and high cheekbones. They had to be related, they looked so much alike. Three long-stemmed white roses. In silky black wrapping paper.

One of them broke out of the huddle and walked toward me. She was so fine and willowy she fluttered like a butterfly as she made her way across the plush carpet. A few unruly strands of hair wisped from her French knot. Bright copper hair. Gleaming hair the color of new pennies.

Pooled sweat streamed to my crotch when I stood up to pay my respects.

"I'm Yvonne Dougherty. And you are . . . ?" Her hand not out-stretched. Her clear amber eyes not smiling.

"I was a friend of Mr Manahan a long time ago. He was a kind person. I will always be grateful I knew Bill." My words lay down on the carpet and died, they were that lifeless. I needed to impro-vise a little more on my standard script. "We were college buddies. I didn't even know he lived in Florida until I saw the obituary."

Old people read obituaries every morning while they eat their bran flakes and drink their prune juice. This is how they find out they are the only people left on the planet who knew them when they were young. I myself had read many an obituary with a survivor's guilty pleasure.

Yvonne arched her thin eyebrows and smiled slightly, and when she held out her hand I took it in my own. Long hard nails and long cool palms. Older than I'd thought, forty-something, but clean and untrammeled.

"Perhaps you don't know, then. Mr Manahan was in some trouble and his family . . ." She tipped her head back to indicate the old lady and the other two women. "His family's not feeling very welcoming right now. They're concerned about privacy issues. Media intrusion. That sort of unpleasantness."

She appraised me to determine whether I understood, and I guess she liked whatever it was she saw in my face, because she seemed to let down her guard a bit. "Be smart about it and avoid showing up at the house. It will get ugly there for anyone who is not, well, a *family* member." She lifted one eyebrow and tilted her head slightly.

When I nodded, she seemed to relax. Her smile was warm and intelligent, keen in some subtle way. "I work for the family as a personal advisor. Bill was my mentor," she said, and I thought I caught a quiver in her voice.

I was still holding her hand. I liked holding it. It made me feel moored.

Of course, eventually I had to let go of her hand. Which I did. And later, after I'd slipped away, I drank that fish bowl of wine.

Now here she was again, her taut thigh practically touching mine. The church was busy for a Wednesday morning at ten. Not crowded, but seats had been taken. There was plenty of empty space, however, in the row upon row of smooth maple pews. No need that I could see for anyone to sit so close to me.

I sniffed at her strawberry-peach perfume, my heart light in my chest. I was enthralled, excited, elated.

Totally pathetic.

"Let us bow our heads now in prayer and remember together a fine husband, father, son, brother, and friend, my own dear friend, Bill Manahan," boomed the priest.

While those at the front of the church complied, I took a moment to check them out. A well-heeled group, they were dressed in dark suits and pressed ties, silk skirts and veiled hats. A woman two rows ahead had a red-cheeked baby propped on her diapered shoulder. The child and I gazed at one another until I looked away, embarrassed at losing a staring contest with a six-month-old.

Yvonne removed her mask and leaned in again. "Father Darcy is full of shit. He hasn't seen Bill in years."

I leaned closer, agreeing to listen, inhaling her evocative perfume.

She tsked. "What a fucking hypocrite that guy is." When I made no response, she whispered, "You're not one of those cloth worshippers, are you?" Her breath was warm and minty against the side of my face. "No, no. I can't see a man like you falling for that shit."

I caught her eye and felt that tingle you get when you make the full connection. We smiled at one another before our eyes eased away.

The priest continued his dull monologue of fundamental righteousness unfettered by doubt. How much easier it must be to live with a mind like that, to abandon logic and free thought, all the conflicts that come with the unanswerable questions.

The mass dragged on. I did not shed a single tear. I was not grieving, not at all. In fact, I was lusting.

Later, when everyone was filing slowly out of the church, Yvonne had her back to me as we exited our pew. Suddenly she stopped, and I bumped into her. She stood there, didn't pull away from me. I hesitated, surprised, her narrow backside pressed against me. Without thinking, I grabbed her thin shoulders and we remained like that for a moment.

To anyone who might've seen us, her action looked like an accident, a stumble or a pause due to overwhelming grief. But to me it was a moment of transcendence. Because I was the one she'd touched, I was the recipient of the rich heat coming from her lanky torso, the musky heat emanating from thousands of invisible pores.

This type of activity made it impossible for me to feel somber and funereal. I certainly wasn't earning my pay. I'd allowed a young woman to distract. In fact, I was wildly distracted.

When she finally moved on, I remained standing by the end of the pew until I saw her exit the church with the others. Then I knelt down and bowed my head, as if in final prayer. My heart throbbed against its bone cage. I was sweating like mad.

The Fifth Rule of Professional Grievers is this: We must remember the cornerstones. The dying need to be reminded of what matters in life, the aspects of living that make it worthwhile. Not the toys, the petty power plays, the little hurts and sleights. Not the minor chords, the catchy memes. But not the bricks and mortar either, the solid materials of the life we build. Nobody forgets all this because this is what we focus on. Too much so, most of us. But at the end? The dying need to be reminded of the invisible, what's there underneath the earth foundation. When our time here is up we need to grasp the score as a whole. We need to visualize the underlying blueprint. The invisible things you can't ever put a finger on. Faith. Love. Friendship. Hope. The cornerstones of a world we build for ourselves every day of our lives.

I detected her sweet scent before I looked over my shoulder to see her coming back up the aisle. She stopped at our pew, removing her hat with its thick veil. She was obviously not a practicing Catholic. No practicing Catholic would rip off her hat in church.

Not that it mattered.

"Aren't you coming?" she demanded, as if we'd known each other for years.

I rose and stepped into the aisle.

"Oh good," she said in a somewhat loud voice.

Her words echoed in the empty church, echoing as if hanging above us in the cavernous atrium. We both looked up. Heavy amber beams of Dade County pine crosshatched overhead, a lovely architectural structure. We admired this together, then looked at one another. An open, naked look.

There was something essential in that moment.

"I thought you could serve as my escort at the lake ceremony," she stated, then took my arm. "I miss having a gentleman to accompany me places I don't want to go."

Arm in arm, we left behind us the comforting darkness of the church for the harsh glare outside. She let go of me to hunt for her sunglasses and pop them on. I did the same.

The bulbous priest stood below us at the foot of the wide staircase, hatless in the cruel sunlight, his pink skull looking tender as a baby's rump. He was maskless, holding court with several elderly parishioners in pale blue masks. Yvonne waved at him and I nodded. He flashed a knowing smile and turned back to his moneyed regulars. His expression was so appropriately mournful I wanted to capture it on film and practice it in front of the mirror.

"If you want to start somewhere, start with Father Darcy," Yvonne said, as we headed to the parking lot. Her long legs matched my stride, although she was nowhere near my height. Maybe five-eight, tall for a woman but small enough to put under my wing. Like Marnie. "He's as dirty as they come and full of secrets about the Manahan family. *And* their friends and relatives."

Unsure what she meant by starting somewhere, I puzzled over her words. But she had grabbed my arm again and I liked that. I said, "No secrets about you, though. Right? The family friar has nothing on you."

When Yvonne smiled she looked like a teenager, one of those beauty magazine girls. White teeth, perfect skin, sparkling eyes. All she needed were pigtails and a cheerleading sweater with a varsity letter on her chest.

Her chest. Now that was another country in need of careful mapping.

But her smile slipped away and she shook her head. "Give me a lift out to the lake and I'll tell you some stories that will blow your fucking mind. Now that Bill's gone, I feel the need to redefine my life. I've got to get away from these fucked-up people."

Her voice shook. Damsel in distress, a red flag. Time for me to run the other way. But of course I didn't. She was trying to tell me something.

We separated when we reached my car, then stared at one another over the rusted rooftop. The glare off the orange metal did weird things to my still tender head. But I couldn't pretend. I looked at her and she looked back and there it was. We had something. An indescribable something.

It scared me how much I wanted that.

I unlocked the doors with a beep, and Yvonne slid into the passenger seat. I took a deep breath, gazing at the startlingly blue sky. Puffs of soft cloud scooted around on a wrinkle-free canvas. I shivered.

Could've been a hangover chill from last night's wine, or maybe it was due to all the sexual tension I was feeling, but I was thinking it was something else entirely. I thought maybe the ice jolt in my veins came from something my body knew but my mind still refused to accept.

The truth.

Fire

WE MET ON the sand. She looked at the sky with me and laughed at my jokes. She made love to me that first night, then held me for hours.

I was all in.

We started seeing one another after that, always sleeping together. But *she* wasn't all in. We were together, yes, but there was someone else in her life. Another man.

Intellectually, I accepted that fact. Yet my heart never did. I struggled emotionally with the reality of the situation. The love triangle. It was too easy for me to picture my lovely Marnie with this other man. A younger man, a wealthy businessman a good deal cooler and significantly more, well, *virile* than I was. Knowing of his existence hurt me, a kaleidoscope of painful images burning in my mind, building in heat and intensity, moving through my entire body, creating ulcerations. Ulcers of the gut and heart. With my depressive personality and tendency to become obsessive, those feelings grew and, eventually, ignited.

I could've confused the interior flame with passion. It certainly made things hotter between us. But it was what it was: jealousy.

See, I loved Marnie the minute I laid eyes on her. Beautiful girl and built like a pin-up. Silky skin, long dark tresses (you had to call a crown of sleek hair like that *tresses*), huge brown eyes. The kind of eyes that looked through your face to the deepest part of your deep matter. And she had the kind of body you'd see on a swimsuit model. Buxom doesn't really describe her. Cantaloupes might be more accurate. There was a reason why I wasn't the only guy to swoon over Marnie. She struck 'em dead all over South Florida.

I could not understand why a young beauty like Marnie would spend time with a deadbeat like me. But I took a chance after our one-night stand and asked her to dinner, and to my surprise she said sure. After our second night together, she basically moved in with me. I don't know why, but she seemed to want to be with me. She made one thing clear, however. The other man was in her life as well and I would have to accept that.

I told her I did. But really, I couldn't. So it burned inside me. Hot, acrid, stinging.

Mr Lasker had been right about the woman in my life. Loving her was killing me. Even though she was no longer in Hollywood at Emerald Day Village, living with me, waiting for me, sleeping with me, I still had her inside of me. I still loved her.

When I thought about all those anxious nights I spent at home, alone, while she was with *him*, I burned. The evenings we were not allowed to talk about after she returned to me, those inflamed my insides. Whenever I thought about her with him, I would feel the internal burn grow hotter. Stronger. And everything would begin to roil. I'd ache for a drink, for a hundred drinks. Whatever it would take to put out the fire.

Mr Lasker had been right about another thing. I could be a real snoop bastard when I wanted to be. I hadn't been spying on him, not at all. But when I fell for Marnie, I indulged in an embarrassing amount of stalking. The Hollywood Public Library became my home away from home. Global wireless access in the privacy of a busy public place. I could spy on her without the fear of getting caught by her.

There were the facts she'd shared with me. Like how she ran her own business, Fleet Feet, a dance studio in a strip mall on Old Dixie Highway a few miles north of town. She'd told me she owned the business. And she'd explained how much she loved dance, teaching dance, and the students she worked with.

But when I checked on her story at the library, surrounded by homeless men muttering to themselves and retirees reading old issues of *The New Yorker*, I found out she'd lied to me. Tucked into my cubicle, I looked up the registered owners of Fleet Feet in the state database: an LLC. I then checked out the owners of the LLC, the digital path narrowing until it led straight up over rocky, dirty terrain, all the way up to the dirty gold mountaintop. And there he stood, the real owner of Fleet Feet, the other man: Mr Untouchable.

That's what I called him: Mr Untouchable.

Robert Gambo lived in a gated community of Spanish McMansions in Boca Raton. Boca fucking Raton. See why I hated that place? I despised that city even before I was a divested asset there, ditched for dead by Milton Lasker.

On the trail of Marnie's other man, and now armed with a name, I continued my snoopery. *Palm Beach Post* articles indicated Robert Gambo was unbelievably wealthy for a thirty-one-year-old with an undergraduate degree in art history from Florida State. A raft of society page images revealed a handsome chiseled face and a body personally trained to perfection and superficially posed in dozens of leisure spreads, his pumped tanning-bed arms wrapped tightly, possessively, around the impossibly thin waists of various semi-celebrity models and actresses.

Sugar daddy, benefactor, philanthropic funder of the arts. Marnie's reason for unexplained departures. I hated him with an adolescent intensity which was exacerbated by time spent alone in the company of a bottle and a glass.

But I didn't confront Marnie with what I knew. I couldn't. I'd promised not to early on, when she'd laid out the ground rules for our relationship. Crazed with lust for her, I was desperate, willing to agree to anything if she'd have me.

Pant pant.

"Seymour, you're a kind man. I appreciate that about you," she'd said that first night.

We lay side by side on the sand, stretched out on a couple of my ratty beach towels under a gleaming white moon. The gentle wind smelled of salt and fresh-caught fish. One of Marnie's long legs wrapped itself around mine and her sharp hip bone prodded my waist. She was cold, she said, snuggling against me for warmth. We had known one another for three hours and I had yet to run my hands over her soft skin. The beach was deserted and my mouth felt incredibly dry. I hadn't made love to a woman in years.

We listened to the hiss and boom of an incoming tide. I was scared shitless of loving Marnie. Not just her, but any woman young enough to be my daughter and gorgeous enough to turn heads when she entered a room. I was out of my league and both of us knew it. She took advantage of my fear and my aching desire, carefully spelling out the parameters of the relationship if we were to move ahead with our intimacy.

"Seymour," she purred, and I was reminded of all the cats I'd known over the years, pretty little cats that ignored me, only rubbing themselves against me when I opened a can of tuna. "I'm very attracted to you. I think we'll be lovers and I know it will be fantastic."

I wasn't so sure. Even though it was probably seventy-five degrees and the palm trees were barely swaying in a delicate off-shore breeze, my teeth were chattering and I was noodle soft.

"If we make love tonight it will be because I feel a certain kind of trust with you. And I need that to be able to love you."

She propped herself up on one elbow to search my face in the faint moon glow.

Actually, the moment wasn't quite that romantic. Because even the dark isn't all that dark anymore. And an overpopulated, overdeveloped place like South Florida is never very dark. There's so much light pollution it's risky to make love on a deserted beach, even when the moon isn't looking.

In the bluish light of midnight in the overdeveloped suburban tropics, Marnie could see everything there was to see on my face. All the frustrated sexual anxiety, the old guy wrinkles, the ageless yearning. The old man fear.

Her fine hair dripped down around her neck and fell into my face, so she flipped it behind her back. Then she said, "I require a level of independence and privacy you might feel uncomfortable with. I know this from past experience, so this is why I'm warning you now, before we get involved. There's a part of my life I cannot let you into, Seymour, no matter how close we become."

She smelled young. The older women I'd dated, they smelled like a stroll through the make-up department at Macy's. Marnie's sleek body emitted a wondrous odor, the tease of the sexual organs of a flowering plant. She smelled like the earth after rain, like the wet sand at our feet. I buried my face in her underarm and breathed deeply.

She pulled away. "This is important, Seymour," she admonished me. "If we're together, I'm sometimes going to go out alone. I'll stay out all night. And when I come back to you, I'm not going to want to talk about where I've been and what I've been doing. I'm going to want you to resist the urge to ask a lot of questions. There are things you won't know about me, about my life. And it must be like this. I will leave you if you can't accept this about me. Tell me now, before we get involved. Can you live like that with me?"

Somewhere down the beach a dog howled. The tide pounded its chest in a primitive way and scraped desperately at the sand. When Marnie leaned down and kissed me, I knew I really had no choice in the matter.

We would be lovers and she would take me down.

Oh yes. Down to the cold dark place Mr Lasker spoke of later. When he was talking about a certain kind of woman, the kind of beautiful woman who had the upper hand in bed and in a man's life. The kind of dazzling young woman willing to take off her clothes for old guys like us. The kind of woman guys like us could never really possess.

Such women were with us for reasons that had nothing to do with romantic love. Neither Mr Lasker nor I was so egotistical that we believed our own PR. We didn't believe for a minute these women loved us for ourselves. An alluring young thing would most certainly have more, shall we say, *practical* reasons for sleeping with balding, aging, limp dicks like us. In Mr Lasker's case, there were the powerful connections, his business success and associated luxurious lifestyle. All that excess.

Understandable. Some women would sleep with a fucking frog if it meant living like a princess.

But what was in it for Marnie, hooking up with a guy like me? I signified nothing in the modern world. Besides, she had her own thing going. Her storefront studio attracted plenty of dance students in a financially rewarding rate of continuous turnover. Marnie dressed nicely, the red dress she wore on our first dinner date an expensive silk sheath from Hong Kong. She lived alone in an upscale high-rise a block off the beach road. When I checked the property appraiser's site online, I found out the two-bedroom condo was in her name and mortgage-free. Although that could've been an arrangement too. Another deal she'd made with Mr Untouchable.

To the outside observer, it might've seemed like *I* was sponging off *her*. I certainly felt like I'd won the lottery.

And oh, what a wondrous prize.

Then I went and fucked it all up. I simply could not understand or accept Marnie's loving devotion, and the other man in her life caused me so much pain and confusion that I acted like a crazed teenager. I wanted to put a going-steady ring on a chain around her neck – with a short, very tight leash attached. I didn't want her out of my sight. I couldn't rationalize my luck and I didn't want it to evaporate in the heat of a Florida afternoon.

I tried to be cool about Marnie's private life but I just couldn't do it. And we both knew it.

Still, she put up with me. Lived with me. Made love to me. Despite my crushing paranoia, my skeptical cross-examinations, my weak and clingy behavior, Marnie stayed with me. She didn't sell off her condo, she didn't truck her furniture to my house, she didn't bring over cartons of clothing and knickknacks. But she spent most nights with me, arriving after work, her body slightly sweaty from dance class, her lovely face pink with excitement and happiness.

I would try to believe it was all for me. But I couldn't.

As soon as she walked in my house I would be on top of her, kissing her damp skin and sliding my fingers into those places that made her tremble. Sometimes we made love on the floor by the front door, that was how juvenile I'd become. After, in various states of undress, we ate dinner together. I cooked big meals for us, fresh fish or shrimp with garlic, bowls of angel hair pasta, tossed salads and steamed broccoli, her favorite menus. We drank good wine with our meals. Most nights she spent in my bed, sometimes waking me at dawn with a soft hand.

She made me happy to be alive.

But I couldn't forget the fact that there was a pinprick in our bubble of happiness. Him, Mr Untouchable. The anxiety his very existence created in my life. The fire in my mind and body. The burning inside that came from furious, frustrated expectation. Waiting for her to leave me. Because some nights she didn't stay with me. Some nights she didn't stay because he called her. And she went. She always went.

There would be a call on her cell phone she simply had to

take, no matter what we were doing at the time. I could have her on the edge of the couch, her head thrown back, one perfect breast in each of my grateful hands, and the cell would go off. There was a ringtone she always answered, a ringtone that became one of the triggers for the acid release in the pit of my stomach. Michael Jackson's *Thriller*. After a month together, I would burn when I heard the first few bars. The old pop song had evolved in my mind into a kind of dirge, a death knell, the sound of intense psychological torture.

She took those calls in the bathroom off the kitchen. After the pocket door slid shut, I would mill around the house, sweat streaming. I felt embarrassed for myself. She caught me numerous times with my ear against the thin door. She'd almost scraped off the side of my face, sliding that door open while I was eavesdropping on her private calls.

But she only laughed at me or scolded me for invading her privacy. But always, always she kissed me goodbye and left. She went to him every time. She would retrieve her discarded clothing, make herself presentable, primp a little in front of the mirror. A peck on the cheek and she was gone.

Some nights the call came when we were in bed, sometimes we were already asleep. She'd bounce up out of bed, get ready. Kiss my lips and go, her heels clacking across the tile to the front door. I'd hear her car start up, drive off into the hot dark night.

On such nights, I always drank too much. I had overdone it in the past, certainly. But I began overdoing my previous excess. I began to drink seriously. Very seriously, with great focus and intention. On the nights when she left me, I slept little or not at all. Instead, I would sit out on the patio breathing the muggy night air, drinking like a professional. A career drinker. Sorry for myself and attempting to drown the self-disgust that came with such feelings.

During this difficult time, Catcher came into my life. He

ventured inside the patio, pretending to ignore me while chasing little brown anoles and geckos around the cement flooring. He liked to snap up the little reptiles, then toy with them in a kind of sick abuse of power. I began feeding him cans of tuna. I hoped this would prove to be a reliable distraction for both of us.

It was. And, after a while, the scrawny cat started to show me some affection. The occasional head bump against an ankle, a rub on a shin, a purr at my gentle petting. Nights spent with Catcher helped defuse my sense of abandonment. Eventually I took him to a local veterinarian, got him his shots and tended to his nails, his teeth. He trusted me, and I reveled in our companionship.

Still, I drank.

Marnie had promised me that time would make things better, but she was wrong. Time made everything worse. We fought more, she stayed away longer. I drank more, and that pushed Marnie further away.

Thus, I found myself in the cold dark place. The fucking cold dark place. Once you get there (and believe me, you don't even know how it happens, but suddenly that's where you find yourself), you stop thinking. You're brain-numb, so you live by your gut. And this is not good for anyone involved, not good at all.

On that last night, the last time I saw Marnie, I started drinking before she got home from the studio. She was late, it was after eleven when she walked in the door. The miso was hot but I hadn't bothered to keep the rest of the dinner going. I'd been out on the patio for more than enough time to put away a decent bottle of pinot noir. One she'd bought for us to share.

Catcher was off somewhere torturing smaller animals. I felt a pang of envy for the primal simplicity of his life.

"Oh, Seymour," Marnie said from the doorway.

She stood there, staring down at the empty bottle on the floor, her face twisted in disappointment. She detested my drinking. She had told me many times how much she despised people who drink alone, drinking fast and hard in order to get slam-drunk. We'd fought about whose fault it was when she came home to find me in a boozy mood. She steadfastly refused to take any of the blame.

"I'm not staying," she said, and turned her back on me.

Before downing the wine, I'd done a couple shots of Jack Daniels. Not enough to dull the pain I was feeling, just enough to smooth the jagged edges. The wine flattened me out. But the disdain in her voice, the hurt I felt knowing she would soon be in another man's bed, all of this hit me with sudden force. The pain seemed to ignite, then explode inside my head. It was like the 4th of July in my brain. And my belly was such a geyser of hot gases, the rest of my body went up in flames.

Boom!

When Marnie left that night, her pretty red dress was torn down the front, her face was swollen with tears, her lovely hair was a mess, and at least one of her nails was broken and bleeding.

Just that morning she had reached for me and, before I had time to open my eyes, she'd straddled me and her head was tossed back, her shining hair a waterfall down her back. We'd been together for eight months and still I was turned on every time she wanted me.

Not that we were all about sex. There was comfort there, too, and caring. We reassured one another that our love would pull us through to another place, a better place. But the way she ignored my questions about her personal life, her secret life, and the way she went back to him every time he called; the way she looked at me when we quarreled about my drinking, the way she looked at me when she came out of the bathroom with her phone and caught me with my head against the door again: these things humiliated me.

My bad feelings got the better of me time after time until there was no better me left.

I'm not proud of myself. I feel terrible about what happened that night. How I forced myself on her. How I stormed into the house and grabbed her from behind. When I kissed her hard, she resisted. She pushed me away. This only enraged me more. I was out of my mind with jealousy and frustration. I couldn't make her love only me. Not when this man had so much control over her life while I couldn't even control my own drinking.

Marnie was shorter than me and I outweighed her by at least sixty pounds. Her body was tightly muscled from years of dance, but her arms were not strong. I pulled her to me and held her to my chest until she stopped struggling. I waited until I felt our heartbeats returning to normal.

We were both silent. My shirt front was wet, from either her breath or her tears, I wasn't sure. I tried to kiss her again but she pulled away.

"Your breath stinks of booze," she said.

That did it. Something shut down in my rational mind, like a light going off, and there was no stopping me. In a kind of mindless fury, I led her into the bedroom and, when she didn't resist, I tried to kiss her mouth one more time. She twisted her head away. I grabbed her dress by the hem and yanked the silk upward until it covered her face. Then I pushed her down on the bed and climbed on top of her.

I was an animal, a monster, but I couldn't stop myself. I didn't want to stop myself. She clung to me, but not with any kind of passion. I was screaming in primal agony. I hardly recognized my own voice.

At some point she tore the dress from her face, and she must have torn open my back then too. She clawed at me, her voice a strangled wail. I felt nothing but my own intensity. Later, in the shower, I found a bloody wedge of her fingernail embedded in my shoulder.

When I came it was furious, violent, a full body explosion. I whooped and roared as the fire ripped free of my gut. The relief was overwhelming. I was panting and dripping, and so was Marnie. The sheets were drenched.

I collapsed on top of her, unable to move my exhausted body from hers. My mind floated above us, staring down at the naked limbs, the entwined torsos, the scattered clothing. I was still wearing my Nikes. My ass looked withered, wrinkled enough to belong in a nursing home. I looked ridiculous. My mind drifted along toward one corner of the ceiling. Something had detached itself and was moving away from me.

That kind of passion was terrifying. The splitting aspect of it made it feel like a warped spiritual experience. It was like a soul war had been waged and the animal part of me had won.

The air conditioner ticked on and the room quickly cooled. I shuddered deeply and Marnie began to shiver.

I rolled off her quivering body and sprawled on my back with my eyes closed. I felt something akin to satiety. A sense of completion. I felt like a different person. In this blissful state, I heard Marnie moving about, retrieving her panties, rearranging her dress, padding barefoot in search of her heels.

When *Thriller* bleated from her purse in the hall, it jolted me out of my reverie. I lay there on my back, my dick still throbbing, an old man with the spirit of a wild animal. I lay there and listened to Marnie talk. She didn't hide in the bathroom this time. I could hear every word she said to him.

"I'm done here," she said. She was, I assumed, speaking to Mr Untouchable. "You win. And you were right. It doesn't matter. All the words, it's bullshit. All of it."

The finality in her voice stung me.

"Be there in forty-five," she said, and hung up.

She stood before me in her torn red dress. Her luxuriant hair was a mass of knots and tangles. Hot pink lipstick smeared down her chin. I sat up and held out my arms. She looked younger, more beautiful than ever.

I knew I could never have her again.

"Seymour," she whispered, not moving toward me, not smiling at me with love and caring in her beautiful face. "I had faith in you. In us. Now it's too late. I'm not coming back this time. I'm not coming back ever."

I couldn't blame her for breaking it off with an old pig like me. But I didn't believe her. Not really. I couldn't. That would have meant pain far beyond my tolerance.

I said, "I love you, Marnie. I do. Even though you run off to see that fuckhead, I still want you here. I want to keep trying to convince you. I could take care of you if you'd let me. But you won't let me."

That's how simple it was in my mind. Love, togetherness, happiness. I was insane. I had no idea.

Marnie smiled sadly at me, then shook her head as if to say, *Will he ever get it?*

I fell back on the bed and passed out. I didn't even hear her leave.

When I opened my eyes it was morning. I hadn't drawn the drapes the night before and the sun was sizzling its way in. The overheated bedroom reeked of sweat and alcohol. Sweated alcohol. I was still wearing my sneakers.

In a daze, I stumbled into the bathroom and retched for a good ten minutes. Ugh. Booze for dinner, what a mistake. My head pounded but I felt strangely light inside, as if a burden had been lifted while I slept. I might have thought the fight with Marnie, the wild sex, what seemed to have been a final split, was all a drunken dream. But then I found the fingernail. I pulled it out of my shoulder while standing under the steaming shower gingerly washing all the places she'd clawed. All the places that hurt.

The pain lingered, then grew worse. Much worse.

On Both Shores

"HELLO? ANYBODY HOME in there?" Yvonne tapped the side of my head.

Her fingers were warm or I'd warmed at their touch. Embarrassed, I smiled at her and apologized. I'd been miles away. Now, apparently, I'd missed our turn.

Yvonne said, "No big deal. All you have to do is bang a U-ey. Do it soon as you can."

She meant a U-turn in Boston-speak.

She went rooting around in her purse while I managed to turn the car around and head back.

"Okay, now take that left. The dirt road," she instructed, lighting a cigarette she'd fished from a crumpled pack of Virginia Slims. As she rolled down her window, a blast of hot air filled the car.

I liked that she hadn't bothered to ask if I minded.

"Sorry," I told her. "My mind wanders sometimes."

Yvonne rolled her eyes and inhaled deeply.

I tried to make amends. "What was it you wanted to talk about?"

No response. After a second deep drag on the cigarette, she tossed it out the window. I watched the butt bounce across the asphalt in the rearview mirror. She hunted around in her Louis Vuitton bag again, pulled out a pack of Dentyne cinnamon. She offered the pack my way before taking a stick for herself. As she unwrapped the gum, Yvonne sighed.

The sun was low in the sky. I adjusted her visor to keep the glare off her face.

"You're incredibly downbeat, but you're an okay guy, Seymour," she said.

I pointed out a small white garbage bag attached to the dash and she tossed in the gum wrapper.

She continued. "Not so many okay guys down here in Florida. At least not in the circle I've been running in." She looked out her window. "And boy, have I been running in fucking circles."

The dirt road weaved, rutting itself deeper into the Everglades. We were crawling along at twenty miles an hour when I caught up to the end of what looked like a long line of even slower moving traffic. I turned to Yvonne and raised my eyebrows. "Well, looks like you're stuck with me for a bit longer. This road wasn't built for funeral processions."

We locked eyes. "This road wasn't built period." I could smell the spicy cinnamon of her gum. "Ever been out to this lake before?"

"Nope." Why would I have? There was nothing out here except thirsty mosquitoes.

"Not too popular with the locals. But very popular with certain people I know in South Florida." She paused for effect, whispered, "A big fucking lake hidden deep in the Glades is a great place to dump the bodies." She chewed her gum hard, deliberately, occasionally suckling it to wring out the flavor. "You know what Mr Manahan was doing for a living during his Florida years?" she asked me.

I didn't even want to guess.

We slowed to a stop. Everyone in front of us had stopped, too, and there were cars pulling up behind us as the line continued to form.

Yvonne rolled up her window, then reached for the radio dial. Jackson Browne filled the air between us. In the quiet of the marsh, it was much too loud.

"The AC's broken, you better roll your window back down," I said.

But when I reached to turn down the volume on the radio she grabbed my hand. "If you want to talk about what's really important, you'd better leave that right where it is. And roll up your window."

She held onto my hand for a moment. I liked it so much I wanted her never to let go.

"The Mob loves South Florida," she said quietly.

I had to lean toward her to hear. She pointed to my window and let go of my hand so I could roll it up, to ensure our discussion remained private. As if anyone was listening out in the middle of the Everglades. Being around the wrong kind of people had made her paranoid.

I knew the feeling.

She said, "They've been coming here since the beginning, back when the robber barons built the railroads and the tourist hotels. Meyer Lansky operated out of Hollywood and Havana, and Boca Raton became a playground for the five families."

She gave me a searching look. I said nothing but I had heard it all before. South Florida was bad but Boston had its share of mobsters too. I'd never been that interested in the gangs of criminals and conmen, the kind the powers that be just seemed to let slide.

Her voice was a low monotone. "You can't fucking blame them for loving it here. Great beaches, good weather, lots of premier restaurants, and a something-for-everyone nightlife. Not to mention the state statutes that prevent the Feds from taking away your homesteaded residence. No matter what heinous crimes you've committed, no matter which laws you've broken, no matter how much fucking money you owe the government, still, you get to keep your mansion. This, of course, explains the 25,000-square-foot castles with the six-car garages you see all over

South Florida. All of them sitting there empty while organized crime protects its ill-gotten gain."

I inched the car forward, thinking about mobsters. Italian Mafiosi, Russian gangsters, all the other ethnic criminal gangs. People of immense wealth from dubious means. It had begun to dawn on me what kind of people my job with Professional Grievers, Inc., was bringing me into contact with. Unpopular people who hired mourners for their own funerals seemed to be the type who'd left a trail of funerals behind them. People who did the dirty work for ethnic crews, for questionable global corporate entities, for corrupt leaders of countries vast and small, for private banks and contractors, for the dark side of the multinationals. As the new face of organized crime, these people were used to living it up. Facing death, they also wanted a grand finale. Even the least popular wanted a big sendoff. Even during a pandemic, they wanted to be honored, adored by the masses.

I could see that. And hence, Professional Grievers, Inc., at your service. "So what exactly did you do for Mr Manahan, Yvonne?"

She stared out her window at the rippling grasslands. The recent rain had brought out the greens to complement the golds, and ibis and egrets white-streaked a blazing blue sky. We both had on mirrored sunglasses, but the relentless sun made us squint.

"You said you were an advisor?" I prompted.

She didn't bother to look my way. As Jefferson Airplane replaced Jackson Browne, she said, "Okay, let's not waste any more time here. I have a good idea what you're after and you must have a pretty clear idea what I've been up to. So let's be frank. Like I told you earlier, I want out. I have a law degree from Harvard and I've got friends, good friends, all over the world. I can disappear like that." She snapped her fingers, but the humid air dulled the sound to a slippery thud. "So I can still have a good life somewhere. Start over as someone else entirely. But that's not how I want my future to look."

I was having trouble following her. I got lost as soon as she said she knew what I was after. Which was what? Rejuvenation? Sex? A replacement for Marnie? Something cool to drink on a hot Florida day? Really, I had no idea what I was after.

She kept talking. "I met Bill at a fundraiser in Brookline. I took the T to the event, he drove me home after. I was fresh out of law school and he had his own real estate firm, an import company, and a penthouse apartment at the Ritz Carlton. I didn't even know people lived like that! He wooed me doggedly, but I'll admit, it didn't take him all that long. The age difference didn't seem to matter. He had so much to give."

I reached in my pocket for my handkerchief and handed it to her. She wiped her eyes. We pulled forward a car length. I was dripping sweat. We needed the windows down, but Yvonne was still explaining whatever it was she believed she had to share with me in the privacy of my sweltering car.

"I loved Bill. Everyone knew that, it was no secret. He added me to his team of legal counselors, and I did serve him in that capacity. I was given an office in Miami where he had his second home. And I had plenty of contract litigation to keep me busy. But really, it was all about Bill. I was so in love with the man."

She paused and we slid forward again. I was tired of looking at the heavily waxed back end of the red Porsche in front of us. But I kept my eyes off her while Yvonne struggled to find the words.

"I'm not a starry-eyed idiot. I knew he had a wife and family, and they knew about me too. After all, we were together for fifteen years." She cleared her throat. "He had two, well, really *three* families, if you know what I mean. Everybody knew about our affair. Nobody seemed to care. As long as I didn't interfere with their deals, they accepted mine. Even his wife, his two daughters."

I remembered the other two long-stem roses from the wake. Daughters, had to be. So where was the wife?

While we sat there, unmoving now, I slipped off my jacket and draped it across the back seat. It was unbearably stifling. Yvonne fanned her face with her hands. Beads of sweat collected along her upper lip.

"Was Bill's wife at the wake?" I asked.

"Bill's wife is a piece of work," Yvonne snapped. "Bill's wife is the daughter of Big Toady Caccitori from Cambridgeport. Bill married into the family. All those years he was her kept man, one of their most successful front men in real estate. He did what he was told, he ran the businesses. He was brilliant, an excellent risk taker. Everyone made mad money while Bill was at the helm. But his wife was just using him. She used him up and then, when he told her he wanted something else, another kind of life, she got rid of him. Permanently."

Uh oh. This sounded terrifyingly familiar. Another undesired asset permanently disposed of? My head felt light. I almost asked how Bill died but my mouth wouldn't form the words. Really, I didn't want to know.

She caught my hesitation, read it as doubt. "Go ahead and look into it. It's all there, all the evidence is there. They don't care. They don't even try to cover this stuff up anymore. The courts, the judges, the local pols, they're all in the big pocket. Everyone is in on the action. Heck, *I* was in on it. I never said a word. I allowed for it, made excuses for what I knew was wrong, all so I could be with Bill. I'm as guilty as the rest of them."

Her peach-frosted lips trembled. She turned away, gazed out her window at the endless vista of unmown grass rippling in the sunlight. Tall, happy, windblown grass. The way grass was meant to be.

Allman Brothers were up next on the rockin' oldies playlist. A snail kite swooped overhead and we watched as it dropped from the cloudless sky toward an unseen target in the marsh.

Yvonne blurted, "I warned Bill she wouldn't let him go. She couldn't. Nobody walks away. That's not how it works. Maybe they let you retire to Florida, but then they relocate the swag and the con. South Florida is the scam and lam capital of the country. This place is dirtier than the fucking back room in a South Boston bar."

I loved women from Boston. They always tell it like it is, no mincing of words. But if Yvonne was saying what I thought she was saying, her words had a life and death definition. A crossword puzzle answer I didn't want to fill in.

"She followed him down here, relocated the business, kept him in it for years. I hung in there, hoping she might let go, but it was no use. She won. There was no getting out for Bill and me. I can tell you stories about her and her family that will give you fucking nightmares. Her hands are like Lady Macbeth's."

The knock on my window shot adrenaline through my body. I jumped in my seat.

A tanned young man grinned in at me. As I turned off the radio and opened the window, he pulled up his neckerchief to cover his nose and mouth.

"Sorry to frighten you, sir," he said. He didn't look sorry. He was practically laughing at me. "Holdup's a fishing event that's taken all the parking spaces in the lot. We're opening up a second lot right now, but we had to get a city okay from one of the higher-ups first. Shouldn't be much longer." He gave a little salute and moved down the line to inform the car behind us.

I eased off the brake and we inched forward, but this time we kept rolling because the traffic finally began to flow. As the line of cars ahead of us advanced the small breeze cooled me off a little.

I said, "Sounds like you need to make a new start for yourself. Get yourself out of Florida."

She nodded. "That's the plan. I'm fully aware it's only a matter of time before I have to pack up and go. Obviously, my job will be terminated. The legal team will be informing me of this fact soon enough. I can break the lease on my apartment, there's no problem there. The asshole landlord has a waiting list. And like I said, I have friends all over. My family's in Massachusetts, and we've got a camp in northern Vermont. Very rural, very rustic. So I have choices. Now that Bill's gone, I'm free to move on with my life."

These brave words were undermined by the sadness in her damp eyes, in her throaty voice. I knew how she felt. I hoped her newfound freedom wouldn't send her into a deep depression. Or on a six-month bender.

I maneuvered the Toyota into the lot, snagging a corner spot in the shade of a shaggy cabbage palm. Cars filled up the spaces around us, doors opening and shutting, voices calling to one another. The humid heat enveloped us. It was like sitting under a pile of freshly laundered linens.

Yvonne sat there, unmoving. "I guess I'm just having trouble accepting the fact Bill's dead. It's like I'm in a bad dream and I keep feeling like I'll wake up and he'll be there, beside me, sleeping. Or lying on his side, watching me sleep. I can't believe we're about to scatter what was once his body into this, this . . . this fucking *fishing hole*."

I didn't comment, but I was wondering how the family got permission to dispose of a dead man's ashes in the Everglades. Maybe they didn't ask. Maybe they just dumped dead bodies here whenever they felt like it.

The cars had stopped pulling into the lot and the other mourners, none wearing masks, were walking west to where the lake was hidden in the tall grass.

I retrieved my jacket from the back seat and said, "Shall we?" I wasn't sure what else to say. I was still in my professional griever role, so potential small talk was limited.

Yvonne looked at me with her huge moist eyes. Marnie, was all I could think.

When I began to blather I couldn't stop myself. "The ancient

79

Greeks believed funerals should be raucous events full of all manner of chaos. Their ceremonies for the dead were loud boisterous affairs which included lots of open sexual expression. Their return to the primal state emphasized the distinction between life and death, between male and female, this world and the other. The Greeks mourned their dead, but they were able to remind themselves of the difference between grieving a dead loved one and being dead themselves. I think they had the right idea."

I'd heard all this from Raymond. I wasn't sure why I chose to share it at that particular moment and immediately I regretted it.

Yvonne didn't respond. The car engine was still ticking; above the sound came the eerie horror-movie cry of a limpkin some distance away.

She examined my face. "Now I'm wondering if you're really a federal agent. Who the fuck *are* you?"

Federal agent? That was even more of a stretch than IRS agent. Why did everyone conclude I was some kind of snoop?

I considered what I should say in response. Did I want to blow my cover and tell the grieving lover I was a hired mourner? No, but I hated to lie to her because I appreciated her honesty. Even if she did associate with mobsters.

The same circle I now appeared to be running in.

"I'm a professional griever," I admitted. "I was hired to attend Mr Manahan's wake and funeral."

To my surprise, Yvonne laughed. "Fucking perfect," she said. "That bitch Mrs Manahan took care of everything, didn't she? I thought there were people at the church I didn't recognize." Her face clouded. "What about this little gathering? Will it be crowded with extras too?"

I had no idea and I told her that. I couldn't distinguish the professional grievers from the real mourners, so I wouldn't be able to tell who was who when we joined everyone out by the lake.

I said, "I can only speak for myself, but I'm here because you asked to come with me. I've been paid to attend the wake and the funeral, but this part of the ceremonies was optional."

As I spoke, I felt the heat crawl up my neck to my cheeks, ashamed to have revealed myself as a fake griever in the face of her heartfelt mourning.

She sighed, then popped open her door. "Okay, so let's get this over with."

Before I could respond she stepped out of the car and headed west.

Gator Land

WE FELL IN behind the black-clad mourners who were wandering down a grassy trail, everyone slapping mosquitoes and scratching at their bites. The sun beat down, unfettered in the cloudless sky. We all walked slowly, trying to keep our shoes from getting mucky as we made our way through marshy land and spiky palmettos to a small clearing.

The lake was calm, and busy with rowboats and other small craft. Participants in the fishing contest. The multi-colored boats sat motionless on the flat lake, glistening in the late afternoon sun. It looked like a Norman Rockwell painting, but the heat was so intense it was difficult to admire the view.

One man in our group turned to face the rest of us. Brother-in-law, maybe? He looked mobbed up. He held the urn while the rest of us assembled in a semicircle around him. Then he began to speak. It was hard to hear him and, frankly, who cared at this point? Our feet were in the muck and the thick, close air smelled like phosphorus, like a giant washing machine. The Everglades reek of fertilizers and runoff from the sugarcane fields and agricultural land upstream. So much for the massive federal clean-up they promised us years ago.

We were facing the lake and the guy with the urn had his back to the water. The setting sun was blood red and the pinkish light ricocheted off the surface, blinding us, even with our sunglasses on. Everyone had their heads bowed against the glare and we were all sweating like mad and the mosquitoes were drilling our exposed flesh. The whole situation was intolerable. It was more than any human could stand. I had to restrain myself from running up and snatching the ashes, heaving the lot of them into the murky water. I wanted to scream at him, *Can you fucking get it over with, please?*

But the guy kept talking. He looked terrible, with his punched-in scary face, his thick neck, his gem-studded pinky rings. A big-mouthed, self-inflated bastard, swollen with his imagined importance, yakking on and on. His greasy black hair, the two-martini gut, the tailored shirt and diamond cuff links. What an asshole.

You know how some people feel the need to turn everything into a political event? To get up and grandstand once they think they've captured everyone's attention? This guy was a real show-boat. The rest of us must've seemed like we were moved by his words but, really, we were blinded by the sun and we were melting in the heat and our blood was being sucked out. We were like zombies, stuck and suffering, while he talked on and on.

I wasn't listening. Instead, I watched Yvonne. Her delicate face floated like a soft cloud above her black silk dress. Her hair fell from its topknot in loose strands that clung to her long neck. Every few seconds she swatted at a mosquito that had gone to work on her arms or legs. She looked like she needed a refreshing breeze from the kind of cool wind that could only be found somewhere very far away. Part of me wanted to be the one to carry her off to just such a place. Another part of me wanted only to get away from her and the problems that surely would remain after years of an affair with a married man. A man married to the underworld. An underworld populated with boring scary assholes like the guy making the speech.

So I wasn't paying attention. That meant I wasn't the first person to notice the gator. In fact, I might have been the last person to see it crawl from the lake and approach. Or next to last. Mr Eulogy kept talking, oblivious to the very end.

Nobody screamed. Nobody warned him. In fact, nobody moved. We all just stared at the slow-moving reptile while the eulogist droned on.

The five-foot long gator was lumpy and a faded black in color. It was trudging low to the ground along the shoreline. It ignored us, blasé and unafraid. Which made me wonder if it was someone's pet caiman, dumped in the Glades by an irresponsible owner. This happens a lot. Monkeys, iguanas, large lizards and snakes are all left to fend for themselves in the manicured wilds of South Florida. Cats, too.

The gator kept moving. I admired its grit. It must be hard for them to adapt to the harsh environment. Unfriendly Florida, with its stark realities of arid overdeveloped land and endless scorching asphalt, too many hostile humans and the havoc they wreak in their ignorant supremacy. I doubted the alligator planned to venture in our direction. It was sniffing around, nose in the muck, probably in search of dinner.

The eulogy continued. The guy must've thought he had his audience in the palm of his hand. He actually paused and grinned at us like a comedian in a nightclub. Was he waiting for applause? Was he done, finally?

He stepped back, held the urn above his head. He wielded it like a trophy. Or a weapon.

That's when all hell broke loose.

The gator turned and looked over at him, at all of us. Then it lunged, moving fast, aiming right for Mr Eulogy's backside. He stood there grinning at us as the reptile shot up into the air behind him.

One reptile coming up against a line-up of citified mobsters, however, turned out to be the losing move for the poor animal.

The mourners had an unfair advantage and they saw it. They whipped out their handguns and took aim.

Mr Eulogy immediately dropped to the ground. Everyone else was locked, stocked, and shooting to kill. Which is exactly what they did.

Yvonne and I were not armed, so she grabbed my hand. She tugged and I followed and soon we were running. We fled back the way we'd come, dashed across the asphalt lot and jumped into my car.

Behind us, the other funeral goers were also in a hurry to escape. Nobody wanted to be hauled into court for shooting handguns in a public park. Shooting a wild animal without a permit was against all sorts of laws. I was with a crowd that preferred not to find themselves in court for *any* reason.

Yvonne crumpled into me and we held each other for a moment. Her hair smelled like fresh-picked strawberries. I inhaled her sweet scent and it calmed me. Enough to start the car and head out ahead of the others. No park rangers or Broward Sheriff's officers descended on us, and within minutes we were heading east toward the interstate.

The sun had wedged itself into its evening slot and the evening had turned cooler. The windows stayed rolled down and the breeze felt great. We didn't talk much until we were almost at the funeral home. When I pulled into the lot, she touched my shoulder.

"Sorry, my car's not here. Can you join me for dinner? Then I won't feel bad about making you drive me home."

When I said I didn't mind taking her home I meant it. Dinner with a lovely woman in mourning appealed to my depressive romantic side. I was a little afraid of being seen with her by the wrong people, however. Her "circle."

Yvonne must have sensed this, because she said, "I know a place. It's private there. Don't worry."

She directed me to an Italian restaurant in a strip mall in her neighborhood. It was small, quiet, off the beaten track. But I couldn't help feeling that everyone was staring at me, wondering why a sweat-stained old guy in a cheap sport coat was dining with the lovely redhead who cried throughout the meal. A few of the dark-haired waiters gave me the once-over more than once. I was so paranoid I didn't dare have a drink: alcohol would only inflame my self-consciousness. I drank iced coffee instead and tried to comfort Yvonne without discouraging her from sharing her emotions. Neither of us ate much.

I called Raymond as soon as I got home. He answered on the second ring.

"Seymour, how did it go?" he asked in his fake jovial voice. "Did you trek out to the Everglades? I imagine it was ludicrously hot out there in the swamp."

He chuckled. Always a good laugh at my expense.

"I need you to explain something, Raymond."

Cell to my ear, I wandered out to the patio with a cold bottle of domestic beer. It was after dark so there was nobody around. No lawn service workers riding by on bulky John Deeres, no neighbors chasing after iguanas and brandishing pellet guns, no old ladies with a plastic bag of dog poop in one hand and a tiny purebred in the other. Emerald Day Village bedded itself by eight p.m. My neighbors took their good night's sleep as seriously as their morning bran.

Trying to remain calm, I asked, "Do you ever *screen* your clients? I mean, are there *any* criteria you might use that would disallow someone dangerous from employing your services? In other words, do you have any idea what you're sending me into when you assign a freelance grief case?"

Catcher appeared, wrapping his furry body around my ankles.

"Slow down, Seymour, please. Tell me what happened. Did

someone try to choke you again? I swear to you, no calls were made from this office."

There was smothered laughter in his voice. The prick.

I sank into the wicker chair, let the cat in my lap. "How reassuring. To know that this time when my life was threatened it *wasn't* due to one of your hot tip phone calls."

Catcher worked at my linen pants, clawing them before settling into a tight ball while I told Raymond what happened by the lake. He stuttered, ultimately saying nothing. I chugged the beer, burped, then launched into an all-out attack.

"Listen to me, Raymond. *You* approached *me* at La Cantina. You've paid me well to attend some pretty routine death ceremonies. I appreciate that, I really do. But then you sent me into the lion's den up in Boca. And after I was left for dead there, you lured me back again, only to cast me into the intimate folds of yet *another* mobster enclave. Why don't you warn me about who I'll be dealing with on these gigs? I mean, Raymond, come on. Is this fair?" My voice sounded cool but I was straining to keep it that way. "I demand double danger pay for this last job. You owe me. And don't you dare laugh."

I heard him snigger on the other end of the line. I was about to hang up on him when he pulled it together. "Sure, sure, Seymour. Danger pay again, no problem. Come in tomorrow morning and I'll make it up to you."

He was trying to sound concerned, but I could hear the smirk behind it. He got a real kick out of this kind of thing, my near misses and run-ins with shady characters. *His* shady clients.

"Raymond, listen to me," I said. "These people are dangerous! Even this tiny old lady I'd talked to at the wake, she pulled out a baby pistol and started firing away! Turns out she's the client. The widow. I had no idea; she wouldn't tell me who she was."

Now I was blathering. I needed another beer, so I dumped Catcher off my lap and headed inside, the phone cradled on my shoulder. "The old bird must've hidden the frigging gun up the sleeve of her funeral dress. She whipped that thing out before I could even catch my breath. Everyone did. I mean, they were *all* armed, Raymond."

I walked through the dark living room to the kitchen before I spoke again. "Armed at a funeral! For what purpose, I am unclear. I don't *want* to be clear on that point. But, my God, it was impressive. The funeral party filled that swamp creature full of holes. It was dead before it hit the ground."

Poor thing.

I cracked open my last beer, letting the froth spill on the floor as I walked back out to the patio. "Do I need to pack protection for this job? Do I need a concealed carry license to work safely as a professional griever? Tell me what I should do, Raymond. Please."

He snorted. "Seymour, look. Wow. That must have been quite the experience. A story you will be telling your friends for years to come. And, like I said, I will agree to the extra costs. Yes, I do think hazard pay is due once again."

"Are you going to answer my question?" I asked.

"Which question?"

Was Raymond really as clueless as he seemed? I chugged, making him wait. Then I placed the empty beer bottle on the floor, another dead soldier next to the first one. Catcher remounted to resettle in my lap.

My voice now sounded as annoyed as I felt. "What I want to know is this: You ever screen your clients? Or do you just assign all the deadly ones to *me*?"

Raymond spoke softly, cajoling me now. "Really, Seymour. You're the only employee who's been experiencing trouble on the job. Professional grievers attend their funerals and pick up their envelopes. No fuss, no muss. I really don't understand why you're ending up with all the clunkers. Really, I don't. You must be inscribing yourself into the sentimental narrative, somehow." He paused and I imagined the snarky upturn of his lips. "But I will leave it up to you to process the subtext in your own way."

The fucker. He was so full of shit. He didn't want to be responsible for what happened to me on the job, obviously. I considered quitting right then and there. Why continue to take chances with his murder-happy clients?

Then I thought about crossword puzzles and cold cups of old coffee, elderly men with plastic hearing aids, aged women with droopy housedresses over dowager's humps. Waste and void, waste and void. I'd had more life in my life since I started the professional griever's job. I didn't want to let that go.

Images flashed through my mind. Yvonne's long legs and smoke-charred laugh. Mr Lasker's aquamarine pool. The rush of adrenaline you get when a predator bares his teeth.

I told Raymond I would be in the next day for my extra pay.

Long after I hung up, Catcher and I were still sitting there in the warm blue night, comforting one another. The palm fronds rustled in an easterly breeze. A confused mockingbird trilled for companionship. My stomach grumbled about too much beer and not enough food. Catcher purred in his sleep.

I thought about how grief doesn't bring you closer to the dead; it cuts you off from them. Dwelling on the loss only makes you feel sorry *for yourself*. And all that feeling sorry for yourself, it drives the dead away. Maybe that's what people were avoiding when they sent others to do their grieving for them. Maybe they wanted their dead to stick around.

I know I did.

Coffee Spoons III

A FEW IDLE COFFEE spoons between funerals, if you don't mind.

Maybe you've begun to wonder about me, sad sack, idle man living in a loneliness box with my loser past and a doubtful future, and you might be asking yourself what roots clutch. Even if you're not wondering about me (because I explained early on that I shall not provide you with the lame details of my questionable past), I have decided to share something about myself here and it is this: I am afraid of death. Mine, yours (albeit less afraid in your instance) and everyone's at once. I fear that big black hole we will, all of us, get sucked into at some point and then . . . And then who knows what happens after that? The unknowingness of death scares me so that I have spent much of my life not thinking about it.

Instead, I drink.

As you may have noticed, this does not work out so well for me. I drink, then I drink too much. I drink so much that I disgust myself. Once I disgust myself enough, then I am willing to relinquish the desire and dry out – only to be sucked back in again and I take another drink. For me this is one of life's black holes that I would prefer to avoid but cannot. It appears inevitable that I must again and again return to the edge and succumb. Every time, it seems, I fall prey to the temptation to float free into the liquid darkness of self-oblivion.

And so the cycle continues.

These are the roots that clutch me. And where did these roots originate? In my genes, my heritage, my ancestry? In my youth, my upbringing, my environment? I can cast blame, that's easy. Been there, done that. But you and I both know the truth lies deeper inside what's left of my soul, a hard truth I feel compelled to blot with booze. And that particular hard truth is a universal truth, a truth I find truly horrid: that of my own mortality.

If this sounds irrational, to replace the fear of death with the alcoholic blackout that so resembles it, well, indeed it is irrational. I will admit to not being rational about booze. Or death. I'm not rational about women, either. This is because, for me, love too is a black hole. With women, certain women, the journey to the jagged edge is alive with sensory delights. The bright spring smell of budding trees and blossoming flowers, the sweet trill of morning birdsong, the blessed cool of long dark nights, the silky feel of naked skin on skin. But the love trail is just another one of life's illusions, a well-trod trail littered with dreamers and fools.

Fools like me. I'm a romantic, as you already know, but a depressed one. If I'd held just a shred of hope for my own future, perhaps I could have overcome my obsession with the bleak horrors of the great unknown to find everyday pleasure in the known.

I had chances to do just that. So many chances.

Fly Seaward,
Seaward Flying

COMPARED TO THE Lasker and Manahan assignments, the next half-dozen grief cases were simple affairs. All virus fatalities, all older people with few mourners. For each job, I showed up, did the work, then departed quietly. No fuss, no muss.

In between gigs, however, I found myself obsessing about Marnie. And, on an increasingly regular basis, I tried to drown the related despair in drink. The next morning I would wake up on the patio in that stubbly, disheveled state that made me cringe with self-loathing. I couldn't stand my own ripe apple smell.

There was a bright note to my sad song: Yvonne called me regularly to chat. She liked to talk to me and I enjoyed listening to her. Our relationship was slightly flirty but platonic and it surprised me how comforting this was. I was still terribly confused about Marnie. When I confided in Yvonne about this, she admitted in a trembling voice she was dealing poorly with deep wounds from her own loss.

Apparently, we'd formed a kind of mutual depression and longing society. That helped me to keep on with the work, and with my own sorry life.

One steamy afternoon Raymond called with a job assignment. "This one is a bit off the mark," he warned me. "No laughing."

I thought that was strange advice. But Raymond himself was quite strange, and more than a bit off the mark, so I signed on and asked him to text me the address for the wake. I had an hour to shower, shave, and inject caffeine into my bloodstream before heading north to super-*über* Manalapan.

The interstate was clotted with stop-and-go traffic jams, speeding cop cars, and irate madmen passing me in the right lane at a hundred miles an hour. I drove the speed limit with my heart in my throat, then pulled off the highway with a sigh of relief. I'd rather not die in a fiery auto crash and, in fact, prefer not to think about them. Goddam I-95 always forces me to think about them.

The address for the wake turned out to be a private home overlooking the ocean. A few luxury cars were parked in the long looping driveway lined with tall palms and evergreens: a stately old Rolls, a new Tesla coupé, a red convertible BMW. When I reached the apex of the drive I saw a couple of unmasked kids in polo shirts and khaki shorts seated by a gushing fountain. I pulled around the standard naked cherub statue spurting water from his stone dicklet and leaned out my open window for the teenaged valet who greeted me.

"Park next door," he said in a cross voice. "This driveway is for family."

Uh oh. Not another *family* funeral. I didn't have the energy for gunfire today. "Where is the homeowner from?" I asked the kid. If he said Jersey or Philly, I thought I would just turn around and head for home.

"Grandma? She's native Floridian," he replied. His eyes were so blue they looked fake. "She's old-fashioned," he admitted with a shrug of his narrow shoulders. "She's making us park cars today. Thinks physical labor will be character building." He rolled his amazing eyes.

I laughed. "So who's the other kid. Your brother?"

"Cousin," he said, then whistled. The second valet jogged over and joined him at my window. Valet *numero uno* instructed the second in command. "Tell this guy where the back lot is. I gotta go take a piss."

When the younger valet leaned in I realized he was a she. "You can give me the keys, I'll park it for you," she said with a bright white smile.

"Isn't that what valets are for?" I asked rhetorically.

She giggled. "Marshall's prickly today. He's in a vile mood because he got his acceptance letter from Yale. Now he thinks he shouldn't have to help out Grandma anymore."

I turned off my engine and handed her my keys. "What about you? Headed for Harvard?"

Her pale face pinkened and she shook her head. Her strawberry blonde hair was cut very short and parted on the side, her body lean and undeveloped. Boyish but fetching, with a smile that was model gorgeous.

"Soon as I turn eighteen, I'm going to New York City to study acting. No matter what my parents say."

"Good plan," I said. She stepped back so I could climb out of the car. "I'll watch for you on Netflix."

She giggled again. Such a pretty sound. "Be careful in there," she warned, turning serious. "Grandma was super devoted to Charles. She's having a hard time with this."

I thanked her for her advice and watched as she drove my Japanese shitbox carefully down the long drive.

When I turned to look at the house, my jaw dropped. What an immense eyesore! The three-story white stone building stretched out in multiple directions with single-story additions that appeared to have been designed by an acid head. The additions were paneled in wood and painted in a shocking array of eye-grabbing colors including periwinkle, tangerine, mocha, teal, and taxicab yellow. The windows were tinted a vomitous shade of green.

I trudged up the white brick walkway, donning my mask as I

went. I couldn't help marveling at the multi-colored rose bushes that lined the entry: purple, red, peach, orange, pink. The property was certainly colorful. Unusual for hoity-toity Manalapan, where residents were expected to be ostentatious but never gaudy.

When I reached the double front doors they opened to reveal a gangly butler in full regalia. He was unmasked and towered over me, blocking the entrance. He held a silver tray in one white-gloved hand and looked down his long patrician nose at me.

"Your name, sir?" he said in rumbling bass voice.

I tried not to laugh but it wasn't easy. "Seymour Allan," I said, stifling a snicker.

He plucked a nametag from the tray, handed it to me. "The wake is being held in the front parlor," he said, avoiding my eyes. "Mrs Hutchinkloss is expecting you."

Well, yes, I thought. After all, she hired me to come today.

I thanked him and entered the foyer, stopping for a moment to pin my nametag to the lapel of my crumpled sport jacket. Removing my sunglasses, I waited for my eyes to adjust to the dim interior light. Then I walked across the black and white tiles, past high tables with giant bouquets of flowers, and down a thickly-carpeted hallway.

The house was musty and silent. Which room was the front parlor? How would I know? I couldn't tell a parlor from a living room or den. My feet were soundless on the plush maroon rug as I stopped now and again to examine one or another of the series of paintings that adorned the hall walls, each one a lifelike oil depicting a German Shepherd in a variety of poses. I guessed Grandma liked dogs.

If only I had been warned just how much she liked her dogs.

The first room I peered into was empty of people. It was deep and dark with several fat leather chairs, a huge mahogany desk, and three walls lined with floor-to-ceiling bookshelves. A reading man could spend years in that room. I noticed a well-stocked wet bar in one corner. *I* could spend years in that room.

It had to be the library, not the parlor, so I moved on.

Light poured into the hall from the next room down, so I took a deep breath and walked in. Whoa. The room was sunken and outfitted hippie-style with loveseats in tie-dye silk, hanging bamboo chairs, and stuffed multi-colored pillows scattered on a buffed pine floor. French doors allowed in the afternoon sunlight, and the view was of an infinity pool and, beyond it, the sparkling Intracoastal Waterway. I marveled for a moment at the passage of a great white yacht that must have cost many millions of dollars. It slid past quietly, vast and outrageous.

The next room down turned out to be – at last! – the front parlor I was seeking. The light in there was exceedingly faint, but I could make out a casket surrounded by huge bouquets at the far end of the room. Armchairs and couches had been arranged in rows before the casket, but nobody sat in them. A small clutch of unmasked people stood by the curtained windows, talking in hushed voices.

A low turnout for poor Charles. I felt sorry for him. There he was with all his worldly wealth but few mourners to grieve for his passing.

I removed my mask as I approached the casket, which looked terribly small. Was Charles a child? My nerves twanged and I started sweating. What would I say to the bereaved? My usual lines wouldn't work if the departed was a child.

I stopped to examine the display of old photographs on a corkboard labeled "Charles Hutchinkloss" in bold blue print. All of the pictures featured a dog, a stately German Shepherd. The dog as a frisky looking puppy, a spry young dog, an old dog curled at someone's feet. In some of the photos the dog was with a woman, in others he was with children. So where was Charles?

Charles was in the casket. Dead as an old dog gets.

I yanked out my handkerchief and coughed into it, trying to cover the bark of laughter that had escaped my lips. No wonder

Raymond had warned me. Then I recalled the pretty valet's advice to take this wake seriously because the hostess was devastated by her recent loss. I stopped snickering and put away my handkerchief.

I'd suffered deeply the loss of my own dogs. This was no laughing matter.

Straightening my back, I knelt down by the casket to show my respect. The familiar odor of wet fur rose to greet me. Charles lay on his side, his profile regal and rigid. A few gray whiskers indicated his age, reminding me he had been a longtime member of the Hutchinkloss family.

I bowed my head.

When I felt a hand on my shoulder, I looked up. An elderly lady with a looming avalanche of snow-white hair atop her small head smiled down at me. "Thank you for coming, Sheldon. I know you were fond of Charles."

Sheldon? Was she kidding or senile? I wasn't sure so I played along. "Yes. This is quite a shock. I'm having trouble recovering from it."

Which was true. I hadn't expected to be paid to mourn a German Shepherd.

She nodded sagely, her eyes moistening. "Indeed. Charles was a dear friend to all. We have been celebrating his life all afternoon. The fireworks will begin at dusk."

Fireworks? Wow, they were going all out. In this case, "it's a dog's life" took on a new twist.

I stood so I could move away from the dead dog. His funky smell was starting to make my eyes water.

Mrs Hutchinkloss reached for my hand and held on. She had cold hands, but her grasp was warm. She said, "It's not legal in Florida to scatter ashes in fireworks. They do it in other countries, but not here. Otherwise, Charles would be launched into the sky tonight. Instead, we will bury him in the yard. You'll stay, won't you, Sheldon?"

"Of course. I am here for the duration," I promised her.

She hugged me then. Nobody hugs these days, not with the virus still in our midst. But the rich are different, immune to common practices. Unsure if she thought I was someone else or was simply pleased with my act, I hugged her back. I could feel her ribs and the sharp bones of her spine. She was frail and had to be at least ninety.

After I arrived, the wake lasted another four hours and fifteen minutes. No one else came to pay their respects, but the valets joined us in the parlor and served drinks. Delicious G & T's. The girl, Pepper, made mine nice and strong, which was kind of her. I sat on one of the leather couches with Grandma's daughter, the mother of the future Yalie, and we chatted about dog breeds. An average-looking middle-aged matron, she was friendly and down to earth. I was introduced to Pepper's parents, and another couple named Bridewater. Nobody asked me how I knew Charles and I was relieved not to have to lie about it.

As the sun set over the Intracoastal, dusting the water in shades of rose and magenta, the butler appeared in the doorway like a phantom. In a bassoon voice, he instructed us to follow him. His gait was as stiff as his personality We all walked slowly down the hall and outside to the pool deck, where he told us to wait for the fireworks to begin.

We stood together on the tile pool deck facing the Intracoastal. A massive navy-blue yacht was moored some fifty feet beyond the Hutchinkloss's dock, and Frank Sinatra songs emanated from giant speakers arrayed on the front deck. A couple of young men dressed in captain's whites set off the fireworks, launching a delightful display of color and light flashing above our heads. We all oohed and awwed.

After maybe ten minutes of booming sky sparklers the display was over. With a salute to the audience, the two men pulled anchor and motored up the waterway.

By the time we re-entered the parlor, the casket was gone. The butler led us out to the side yard for the burial. His Lurchy demeanor was perfect for a funeral. I wondered if he worked for Raymond rather than Mrs Hutchinkloss.

We stood together on the manicured lawn in a stand of slash pine. It was dark, but you could see the black shadows of headstones. Eight small gravestones, each labeled with a single name. Ralph. Buster. Fred. Roger.

Marshall's mother whispered in my ear. "She buries all her pets here. When she passes, she wants to be buried here as well."

I lifted an eyebrow. "Is that legal? Are you allowed to be buried on a suburban property?"

"In Manalapan?" She snorted. "Even fireworks are illegal here. But, that said, anything is allowed as long as you know whom to pay off."

I laughed. Corruption is a way of life in South Florida.

As the casket was lowered into a pre-dug hole, a priest or reverend materialized. He wore the white collar and looked the part. After he had spoken for a few minutes about the soul of the deceased and the better place Charles was now in, the man faded back into the pines. Mrs Hutchinkloss wept loudly while her relatives comforted her.

All in all, it was a fine send-off for a well-loved member of a very nice family. The dog had lived a good life. He had been a loving pet and had been loved in return.

My car was waiting for me by the burbling fountain. The valet girl jumped up from where she was sitting next to the peeing statue.

"Thanks for coming," she said, flashing me her heart-stopping smile. "I'm sure my grandmother appreciates it."

"Charles too," I said. "Woof woof."

She laughed, which made me smile. Nothing warms the heart like the sound of a pretty girl's laughter.

On the long drive back to Hollywood, I wondered why I had been sent to a dog's funeral. I wasn't insulted, just curious. But I didn't want to ask Raymond about it. In fact, I decided I wouldn't mention it. Instead, I would accept the payment due and thank him, then move on to the next assignment. This time, I wouldn't give Raymond the pleasure of knowing he'd set me up as the fool, that he'd fucked with me once again.

The next day I called Yvonne to tell her about the dog funeral. I exaggerated the ludicrous parts of the story just to hear her laugh.

Fear in a Handful of Dust

A FEW WEEKS LATER, a call from Raymond woke me before noon. I was not hung over (for a change), but I *was* beaten down. The summer heat and stifling humidity had me by the throat, while the day-to-day boredom of pandemic life throttled me. Plus, I was lost in the wasteland of my own sadness. My bedroom smelled like a man's loneliness and it embarrassed me. So I accepted without hesitation the offer of a day's work, grateful for the opportunity to escape my solo funk. And I readily agreed to drive five hours north for what Raymond called a "natural" funeral in the boonies of rural Florida.

Personally, I couldn't see anything natural about dead people. But I was so anxious for something to do which didn't involve alcohol and self-pity that I didn't stop to ask Raymond what he meant.

"I'll do it," I said, reaching for the glass of warm water on the night table beside my bed. "But Grotonville is bumfuck and it's a hike. Do I get travel expenses?"

"Of course. If you wish to stay the night, I can make arrangements for a room in one of the old Victorian B & B's located in the center of town. Or what passes for a town up there in the hicky sticks." Raymond sniffed. "Unless you'd prefer to return tonight once the burial is over?"

I stretched for a moment, then sat up. Ten hours in my rusted-out Toyota seemed like too much to ask of it. "How about you rent me a road-worthy vehicle for the day?" I suggested. "Then I can make it up there and back in a reasonable amount of time."

A Suburban or an Explorer would do. If I needed to pull over in a rest area for some shut-eye, there'd be an acceptable level of comfort.

Raymond said he'd have a rental car waiting for me at the Hertz office in downtown Hollywood. "But the funeral starts at dusk so you need to hop to it, Seymour."

I slid out of bed to pull myself together and get on the road.

Thirty-five minutes later I cruised onto the interstate in a murdered-out vehicle, a black Escalade with extra-dark tint. The thing was a tank. I rolled over everyone else on I-95, no longer nervous about the crazy drivers. For once, *I* was the monster other drivers feared.

I made it to the city of Gainesville in record time, but Google Maps failed me once I entered the no man's land northwest of the university. I drove slowly on a maze of back roads, marveling at the rural expanse, the flat vistas of cropland with scattered trailers, the slow-moving cows and occasional mule, the wide blue sky with huge wads of pure white cloud you could almost touch.

When the sun sank low in the sky I realized I was going to be late. I appeared to be driving in circles over a mess of rutted roads. I pulled over and idled beside a circle of buzzards feasting on something bloody and torn. I leaned out the window to talk to an elderly man in a surgical mask and a plastic face shield. He was hunched over a battered mailbox.

"Excuse me, sir? Can you direct me to the Grotonville Nature Preserve?"

He turned and stared up at me. His back was shaped like a "C", most likely from years of labor on the acres of farmland spread out around us, but his eyes were still bright and exceedingly sharp. "I can. But I ain't so sure I should," he said. "What you got in the back there?"

I had nothing in the car and I told him so, thinking he must be demented or paranoid or both.

"I'm attending a burial and they're expecting me," I said.

He smirked. "I bet they are." After he gave me directions, which were complicated but blessedly brief, I thanked him.

He shook his head, frowning. "Now don't think I'm gonna talk to anybody 'cause I keeps to myself," he said before I pulled away.

Definitely demented.

With some difficulty but no more wrong turns I found the sign and the wooded entrance to the preserve. The road in was narrow but built of fairly smooth asphalt, and after a mile or so it ended in a small parking lot. Four SUVs were parked there, all of them murdered out. What a strange coincidence, I thought, as I parked in the row of black, heavily tinted vehicles.

The sole car in the lot stood out, a sleek gray Maserati. A tall, hot-looking blonde in a tight black dress stood beside it, locking up.

The sun was tucked somewhere behind the trees so the lingering light lay low over the preserve, which was mainly composed of scrub and live oaks. From this point on, I had scant directions. *Take the trail to the funeral* was the only information I had. So I jumped out of the Cadillac and followed the big blonde, who walked fast despite her spike heels. I hurried to catch up with her as she sped down the semi-muddy trail, her fat Dior purse swinging wildly at her side. Her narrow hips swayed like a pendulum in her long silky skirt, and I found the view mesmerizing. Finally I stopped gawking and walked up beside her. I needed to make sure we were going to the same place.

Neither of us wore masks. On grieving jobs I always dressed to blend, not to stand out.

"Excuse me, but is this the way to the burial ground?" I asked, panting a little.

She turned to look at me. Oh dear. The wig was obvious in a close-up, her hairline a dark seam. The makeup had been plastered on so thick it looked clownish. His beard was beyond a five o'clock shadow and fast approaching ten p.m. He wasn't really trying to pass for female, was he?

He grinned at me. "Funny, pal. You with Dasher's crew?"

Dasher's *crew*? I said I was, although that certainly would not be the term I would have chosen. I considered myself a freelance professional, not a member of a scull team. I wasn't a team player of any kind.

"This guy, he's fucken *uuuuuge*," my guide said. His accent was Newark, his manner exceedingly gruff. I didn't know what to say. His outfit really had my head in a spin. "We need all the help we can get, man," he added, speeding up the slight incline. The land around us was marshy and I spotted herons and egrets standing in the shallow water off the trail. "You ever been here before?"

I said I hadn't. "Never been to a natural burial either," I admitted.

He laughed at that.

When we arrived at the top of the small hill I saw the vista below us included what had to be thousands of acres of upland mixed forest. Immediately to our west in one of the many oak hammocks stood a tight group of mourners. The last of the daylight leaked though the thick stand, but I couldn't see what the grievers were doing. They seemed to be active, however, moving around, some bent over, others lifting something. What they were *not* doing was standing in a circle to listen to a man of the cloth provide the final blessing for the newly departed.

Perhaps I wasn't late after all.

"Are we on time?" I asked my companion.

He glanced at me with an odd expression on his face, part

skepticism, part amusement. "Don't worry about it, bro. S'all under control. He's just extra man, that's all."

Extra man?

Blondie led the way to the mourners with me at his heels.

The first thing I noticed was that the group was all male. And nobody was dressed for a funeral. I was the only attendee in dress slacks and a sport jacket. The other mourners wore jeans and tee shirts. Except, of course, my guide, resplendent in his black dress and fuck-me pumps.

"Yo," he called out as we drew nearer.

Everyone turned, putting a halt to all the mysterious activity.

"I brought reinforcements," my friend said, pointing to me. "I'm not dressed for the occasion myself, so you'll have to excuse me this time."

The men laughed. Somebody yelled, "Fuck you, Tony." Another guy said, "Enough already. We gotta get this guy in the fucken ground."

These were the mourners? It sure didn't look like it. They certainly didn't display the appropriate attitude such solemn occasions normally call for. Were they grave diggers? That too seemed unlikely.

What had Raymond gotten me into this time I wondered, as I stepped forward to see what the men were doing.

Six men with shovels resumed their work. Apparently they were digging the grave. And what a grave it was. The hole in the mucky Florida soil had to be six feet wide and, at that point, about four feet deep. They were aiming for six by six, apparently. The grave was going to be huge. Or *'uuuuuge*, as my new friend would say.

Was this normal preparation for a natural burial? I'd googled the subject on my phone while waiting for the Hertz employee to bring the rental car to the front of the lot. According to Wiki, natural (or "green") funerals were allowed in certain states and counties. The rules and legal restrictions varied from place to place, but most made it possible to bury the dead without a casket or embalming. Body, hole, dirt, dust. Around the US many of the natural burial grounds were located on preserved acreage, which provided a kind of permanence for the bereaved and helped save the land from future development. Other natural burial grounds were situated on private property, either in special areas set aside in cemeteries, or on land a landowner had decided to preserve specifically for this purpose.

According to social media, green burials were trending.

Personally, I didn't want to think about bodies dumped in holes in the ground with nothing to protect them from the elements, the bugs and worms, the inevitable rot. But research indicated the rate of decay for a body in the ground was not much different from that of an embalmed body in a pine box. A metal casket could slow things down, but not by much. And in the end, did it really matter?

I didn't want to think about it.

When my eyes adjusted to the darkness that had settled in around us I realized that what I'd assumed to be a second pile of grave dirt was, in actuality, an immense man. An immense dead man.

He was on his back, arms by his sides, clothed in what looked like a big black curtain that had been wrapped tightly around his bulk. I'm not good at guessing body weights, especially for corpses, but I would have estimated that one at four hundred pounds. Minimum.

Extra man. Now I understood. And he would have to be lifted into the hole. The big fucken hole.

With a sigh of resignation, I took off my jacket and draped it over a low tree branch. Immediately, hungry mosquitos drilled into my bare forearms. My ears and neck already had itchy welts.

I stepped up. With a low mutter of gratitude, one of the men handed me his shovel. He was drenched in sweat, his shirt plastered to his muscular torso. The gun tucked in the back of his waistband did not surprise me, because by that time I knew what this was. Not a natural burial per se, certainly not a normal funeral. With Raymond Dasher and Professional Grievers, Inc., there *were* no normal funerals. And this was a body disposal, most likely a murdered body disposal.

Just like my Escalade, the big guy was murdered out. And now *I* was an accessory after the fact.

Shaking my head in self-disgust at my naiveté, my stupidity for continuing to take assignments from Raymond C. Dasher, I dug in. The soil was thick and damp, heavy lifting. But I worked it. I dug and dug. Mindless, oblivious to the chatter of the men around me – they were only mobsters, just stone-cold killers armed with loaded handguns – I kept on digging. I dug until the sweat streamed down my face, my ribcage, my back, my thighs. I dug until my left palm blistered and bled. After I had wrapped my handkerchief around that hand, I dug some more.

There were seven of us not counting the one in drag. Together but with much difficulty we managed to lift, shove and roll the massive body into the deep and muddy hole. After he had landed – with a resounding splat – we high-fived each other. It took us another hour to fill in the hole and pack down the wet dirt. Finally we covered the fresh grave with branches and brush, leaves and acorns, pebbles and small rocks, until the burial area blended in nicely with the surrounding environment.

Very much a natural burial. Except for the fact the gravediggers were most likely murderers, and the body that of a murder victim.

Also, in this case, there was no marker. Obviously, no one would be coming here to mourn their loss. Their very big loss.

As we worked, the night had closed in around us. The hum of mosquitos had died down and the crickets were singing from the trees while tiny bats swooped overhead. An arc of juvenile egrets swept upwards with a whoosh and flew off together. The moon rose in a silver sliver and bright stars popped out across the black sky.

The men talked among themselves, joking around and laughing. When I finished up I stood off to the side, scratching my bug bites while they smoked cigarettes and chatted. I tuned them out. I didn't want to know. All I wanted was to get away from them in one piece. But I was afraid to leave. What if they didn't let me go? What if they saw me as an outsider, a witness to their crime?

I needn't have worried. My friend in drag pointed to me and reminded his peers, "This guy's on the clock. He's gotta go."

All the men shook my sore hand and a few slugged me on my sore shoulders. They were dirty, sweaty, rough-looking gangsters, but okay guys.

My guide and I retraced our steps over the trail to the lot. We halted once to allow a hunching bobcat to scurry past, a fresh-killed rabbit in its mouth. Barred owls swooped down, capturing rodents in the tall prairie grass. The hooting of great horned owls, their deadliest enemies, was seriously creepy.

When we arrived back at the well-lit parking area I still felt nervous. I headed for the SUV, hoping my new mobster pal wouldn't shoot me in the back before I reached the safety it offered.

He didn't. He did call out to me, however. "Hey! Aren't you gonna ask me?"

When I turned around, he was standing with his hands on his hips, head cocked to the side. The wig hair shone a brilliant gold in the light of the street-lamp overhead.

Did he want me to ask him who the dead guy was? How he'd died? If they'd murdered him? Why they were allowing me to leave after witnessing what they'd done?

My legs felt weak and I stuttered for a few seconds before he interrupted me.

"I'm transitioning, bro. But it's early yet. I got a long ways to go."

I managed to wish him good luck before my knees started

to shake. With much effort, I lifted my exhausted, bitten-up and nerve-wracked body into the comfortable front seat of the Cadillac.

It was dawn when I pulled up to my little house in Hollywood. I was physically exhausted but mentally alert, and feeling very much alive. While I drove the dirt roads and sped down the empty highway, I had been thinking about what I would say to Raymond. He had paid me to help criminals involved in a criminal endeavor – if that's what it was – but of course that's what it was! He'd made me an accessory after the fact, but he was himself complicit in the crime as well.

Once in my driveway, I shut off the engine and lay back in the leather seat. What the hell? How could Raymond do that to his employee? Why would he do something like that to me? Put me in danger. Send me into a den of wolves, a crew of murderers, without preparing me in any way whatsoever. Expose me to criminal prosecution. Or death by mobster.

But when I walked into my house, stripped off my filthy clothes, and stepped into a steaming hot shower, I felt good.

Damn good.

There is Not Enough Silence

F OUR DAYS AFTER the "natural burial" in Grotonville my bites had disappeared and the blisters were mostly healed, but I was already feeling listless again. My fears about the danger I'd been in had faded and I wanted another assignment. I needed one.

By reflecting on the work I was doing for Raymond, I had come to know myself better. The people and situations these gigs exposed me to were doing something for me. They were making me *feel.*

So I swung by Raymond's office en route to the discount liquor store on North Federal. If he had work for me, I would cancel my shopping trip. If he didn't, well, then I had nothing better to do.

I hiked up the stairs, my legs still a little stiff from all the digging and lifting and squatting over the giant grave. The second floor of Raymond's building was quiet, and as usual his reception area not manned. I texted him from the front desk and heard his phone ding at the far end of the hall. He responded to my text by sticking his head out of his office door and waving at me, beckoning me to join him.

When I walked into his cool, dark office, Raymond was standing by the shuttered window talking on the phone. "Yes, of course, I understand," he said, rolling his eyes at me. "Of course, the utmost discretion."

He was dressed in his usual garb, the expensive suit, the

starched shirt and silk tie, the polished Italian shoes. Nodding and smiling, he pointed with his chin to the two chairs in front of his desk. I sank into one, embarrassed to be barging in on him while simultaneously hoping he was speaking to a client who would need my immediate services.

"This afternoon at three. Fine. You are very welcome," Raymond finished, then said goodbye before clicking off. He turned to me. "Looking for an assignment?" he asked, a smug smile tickling his lips. "Something dreary and depressing to chase away the summertime blues?"

He was lording it over me, so I was tempted to say I wasn't interested, I'd had enough gangland activity to last me a lifetime. But I just didn't have it in me to argue with the man. He knew I was desperate for work and I probably seemed it when I said, "I'll take the gig you were discussing just now, if that's okay."

He slid into his desk chair and stared down at the smooth oak desktop. It was clean, of course, with no paperwork to mar the pristine surface. "I'm not sure you'll want this particular job, Seymour. It's a straight pickup and delivery. Not your typical wake or funeral service."

I laughed. "Sounds so easy. Why do I suspect there's some sort of catch? Might there be illegal activity involved?"

He tsked. "Now, now. You shouldn't be so judgmental regarding our clientele. People of all types require our services and we must respect their end-of-life needs."

I respected them, all right. I just didn't want to find myself in prison because of them. Or in need of funeral services myself.

I managed to hold my tongue while Raymond provided the particulars of the case. When he told me the payment fee was six hundred dollars, I stood up. "Done. Text me the addresses."

He chuckled. "Okay, then. It should be a simple job. You should be in and out within a few hours. Then you'll be glad you dropped by today."

I wouldn't bet on that. Not with the track record I already had with Professional Grievers, Inc. But I was pleased to have work that would keep me busy, even if it was only for the afternoon. So I thanked him, then thanked him again when he paid me for the Grotonville gig.

I skipped the liquor store and went home to change my clothes. Even though the gig didn't involve a funeral, I wanted to look professional. I put on a freshly ironed shirt and took my sport coat with me.

The address Raymond had texted me for the pickup was a jewelry store on Los Olas in Fort Lauderdale. The drop-off was near Okeechobee at a business called Florida Sweets. I googled the business and found out it was a sugar cane farm and mill located deep in the Everglades.

Weird. But my job was not to wonder why, just do the work and try not to die. Or something like that.

When I started up the Toyota the engine chugged a little before catching. I hoped it would make it into the heart of the Glades and back. But I didn't want to ask Raymond to rent a car for me again so, fingers crossed, I pulled out on to Federal Highway. Then I drove north to Fort Liquordale, wondering what jewelry and sugar cane farming could possibly have to do with Professional Grievers, Inc.

The jewelry store had a parking lot in the back, so I left the stuttering car there and walked through the brick alley to the front of the building. The display in the window was Tiffany-esque, with crushed velvet pillows adorned with oversized diamond rings, sparkling emerald brooches, and long strands of plump pearls.

As soon as I entered the frigid air-conditioned store I could see I was underdressed for the elite ambiance. The clients were elderly stiffs in pressed suits, their wives with helmet hair and lifted faces, all with masks that did not conceal their bitter expressions.

I waited in an embroidered armchair while the shoppers gave the man behind the counter a hard time about prices, jewelry settings, a recent city council meeting they didn't like, and the upcoming local elections in which nobody they approved of was running for office.

I felt sorry for the poor salesman. What a terrible life, catering to people with nothing positive to say.

When the last of the senior set had limped out, the man behind the counter pulled his mask down around his neck to flash me an exhausted half-smile. A wiry fellow with a gray handlebar mustache and matching eyebrows, he spoke in a deep, cultured voice. "So sorry for your wait. How may I help you, sir?"

I got up and approached him, saying, "Here to pick up the delivery for Florida Sweets."

I didn't tell him I had no idea what that might consist of, but his reaction was, in hindsight, predictable. His smile faded and he stepped back from the glass case. His face paled and he looked down, his voice shaking a little when he said, "Oh goodness, why didn't you say so as soon as you walked in? I'll get that for you at once, sir. At once."

Remasked and sheepish, he scurried away.

I wondered what exactly I might be retrieving. Stolen gems? Drugs? Non-native species like tarantulas preserved in amber? I was tempted to walk out of the store and keep going, but this was the most excitement I'd had since Grotonville. So I waited for the jeweler, perusing the glass cases, staring at the striking array of luxurious bling. Thick gold bangle bracelets, delicate silver crosses encased in tiny diamonds, emerald- and ruby-studded watches. Everything sparkling and, I was sure, crazy expensive. You can always tell when there are no price tags in sight.

The package he held in his hands when he returned from the back of the store was about the size of a coffee can. In fact, it looked like a coffee can, but it was a burnished copper with a matching lid. The jeweler handed it to me with exaggerated care. It was surprisingly heavy.

Next he held up a rather large star-shaped pendant on a long silver chain. The star was an odd color and texture, a dusty golden brown, kind of splotchy. Beautiful in its own strange way: I'd never seen anything quite like it before. He placed the necklace in a black box lined with white velveteen. After he had snapped the jewelry box closed he handed that to me as well.

Eyes downcast, he said, "Please tell Mr Fantaticaria the remains that were not used in the pendant are in the urn. He may wish to keep the rest of her ashes, or scatter them, or use them in some other way. The pendant is approximately ninety percent bone ash. It will last forever."

Swallowing the bile that had inched up my throat, I tried to hide my surging disgust. I sure hoped the widower wasn't going to wear this necklace made from his dead wife's bones.

I asked, "Do you make other items from cremains?" I was horrified but kind of curious. "Like rings and things?"

His eyes met mine and he nodded. "Yes, on occasion. When our clients request them. As you can imagine, it's not a large part of our business. We specialize in unique handmade jewelry designs and most of the work we do does not include cremation ash." He raised his luxurious eyebrows. "But we would do anything for Mr Fantaticaria. He's been a loyal customer for more than forty years."

He studied my face, which might have blanched, I wasn't sure. I was feeling kind of woozy. The jewelry box burned hot in my hand, as if it had just come out of a giant oven. I slid it into my jacket pocket. It was freaking me out.

The jeweler said, "Please tell him again how sorry we are for his loss."

That I could do; and handing over the urn: not a problem. Sharing with him a piece of jewelry made from his deceased wife's cremated remains? That wasn't going to be so easy.

But I nodded at the jeweler and promised him I would pass on his messages, along with the two items he had given me. Then I hurried outside and Google-mapped the address in the Everglades. The car whirred and spat, but eventually the engine turned over.

I took the back route, heading west first. The suburban sprawl of South Florida quickly disappeared, replaced by acres of tall marshy grass. A vast sea of grassland. The Glades has a unique ecosystem, like nowhere else in the world. It's wet and it's grassy simultaneously. Environmental activist and revered author Marjorie Stoneman Douglas dubbed it *the river of grass*. This is exactly the right description of how it seems to me.

In the afternoon sunlight it was a golden brown with wide swathes of brilliant green. I drove past black water canals, some with alligators sunning on the muddy banks. I passed scores of water birds, anhingas drying out their wings, osprey on telephone poles waiting to swoop down for flying fish, hawks of various kinds. And my favorite, the belted kingfishers with their pointy crowns and sharp bills.

As I drove, windows down, mask off, I let the hot air wash against my face. Soon enough, I felt better. Once I got rid of the creepy bone ash necklace I could go home and relax. Have a drink or three.

When I arrived at the address I'd been given for the sugar company, I was surprised to find massive cement block buildings surrounded by a high electric fence. The fence was plastered with neon red warning signs. The place was fortified like a prison. I drove up to the guard gate and stopped to talk to the security personnel. Was sugar in need of this much protection? What was with all the security?

A young black guy took my name. He was decked out in a military-style uniform complete with a shoulder harness in which a big fat Glock had been slung. He made a call from his glass booth. Minutes later, he returned and leaned in my car window. His N-95 was huge: it resembled a gas mask.

"Sorry, sir, Mr Fantaticaria's not here today."

What?

I was tempted to hand the kid the two unpleasant delivery items and skedaddle, but that would mean not completing the assignment. Raymond would be very upset. And I wouldn't feel right giving such personal materials to a security guard.

"Can you call him and find out where he wants me to leave the delivery?" I asked.

While the guy was back in his tiny office, I called Raymond.

"Take them to his home," he told me. "I'll advise him you'll be late. His home address is in Palm Beach, which is just over an hour from where you are now. I'll pay you a bonus fee, of course, for the additional time and mileage."

I didn't object. But I did ask him about the security.

"Don't be naïve, Seymour," he said curtly. "What if someone, one of America's enemies, decided to poison our sugar supply?"

I laughed. How ridiculous! They were obviously hiding something in there. Like how much polluting they were doing, or how bad their product was for consumers. I would have argued but Raymond had already disconnected.

The security kid came back to my window with an address on a slip of paper. "He's expecting you, sir."

I reset my phone with the new address. Then I drove past miles and acres and miles of acres of sugar cane fields. This early in the season there was little to see but an endless parade of stalks only a foot high. But I knew that by late fall the cane would be tall and thick, ready for harvest. The Fantaticaria family owns the majority of the very lucrative US sugar business. They're multi-billionaires. Their other claim to fame? They're the chief polluters of Florida's land and waterways.

Maybe they were protecting themselves from angry environmental activists, I thought. Or others seeking revenge. Plenty of people had been exploited by the sugar industry, including the Fantaticarias' workers and their customers. Sugar itself was responsible for a lot of heartache, obesity, tooth decay and. . . . death.

I certainly did not want to meet the company founder and CEO in person, no thank you, sir. But I reassured myself I would be dropping off the delivery to a minion like myself. Still, the sick feeling returned and my mood soured as I continued to pass by the unending fields. Hundreds of acres owned by a family whose greed had caused significant loss of flora and fauna, and whose stubborn refusal to take responsibility for their waste constituted a serious threat to the people of South Florida.

By the time I arrived in ritzy Palm Beach I was tired of driving around with a bunch of cremains and I was angry. I pictured myself speeding by the rich man's estate and tossing the wife's ashes on to what was sure to be a vast green lawn pumped full of fertilizers and pesticides.

I had worked myself into quite a state; and then, as I rumbled across the bridge to the beach road, my head full of righteous ire and my hands tight on the wheel, the car sputtered. It chugged, bucking, then it slowed and died.

Goddam it!

I rolled over to the side of the road just beyond the bridge and parked on the swale. After I had texted Raymond I got out of the car and propped up the hood. The engine looked like it always did: complicated and foreign. So I stood there like an idiot while rush hour traffic crawled past me, everyone gawking.

Raymond texted back: the Fantaticarias' limo would pick me up momentarily. Less than a minute later, a sleek black Lincoln Town Car pulled up beside me.

The driver's side window slid down silently. "You almost made it," the man said with a friendly grin. "Look, man. Chester's gonna take care of the car for you. Climb in back and I'll take you to the house."

A small Hispanic man with long hair and a graying beard exited the passenger seat of the limo and waved at me. "No worries, man. I fix your car."

While he began to examine the engine, I described my car's symptoms. Chester nodded, his unmasked face serious. "No worries, no worries," he promised me.

Easy for him to say. He had a limo driver on hand.

I grabbed the urn and pendant from the front seat of my dead-beat car and settled into the plush leather of the limo. The driver, a burly guy dressed in tennis whites, introduced himself as Franklin and told me to relax, he'd have us there in under five. He wasn't kidding, the house was just up the street. Traveling the length of the marble driveway took about as long as the ride from the bridge. I could've walked.

I felt even more embarrassed than I had on the bridge; but my anger had eased. Now I was in Mr Fantaticaria's debt. I hoped I wasn't expected to wear a mask, as I had left mine dangling on the rearview.

The house was a four-story monstrosity with a flat roof and narrow windows like buttonhole slits. *Museum modern,* the architects called the popular design. Ugly is what I called it. A helicopter pad was located on the west side, Franklin explained, tennis courts to the north, Olympic pool to the south, and a hundred-and-twenty-foot yacht parked out front on the Atlantic Ocean.

I would have been impressed, except that all I could think about was the toxic algae that killed off coral and fish, sea turtles and dolphins, and caused respiratory illnesses in vulnerable Florida residents living by the waterways. Dogs had died in one recent blue-green algae infestation. These almost annual environmental crises were caused by runoff from the fertilizers and pesticides used by the sugar cane industry.

We circled around the requisite fountain. I felt like I was entering the maw of the beast. Entering with the ashes of his dead. Like in some Greek myth.

Franklin dropped me off by a portico that resembled the one at the White House, and I walked up the white marble steps. I was planning to hand the packages to the butler or maid, then walk back to my car and see how Chester was making out. But when I got to the double doors they opened and there he was. Mr Fantaticaria.

Tall, fat, dark, handsome and dressed in a maroon smoking jacket and matching slippers, he greeted me by name, flashing a warm smile. To my surprise, he welcomed me into his home with a hug and European-style cheek kisses. Totally against all pandemic warnings and virus safety protocols.

"I am so sorry for all your trouble, Seymour," he said. "It is my fault you were sent to my office instead of my home. And so it is my fault you now have car trouble."

He slid an arm around my shoulder and guided me into the foyer, a massive open space under a fifty-foot ceiling. I stared up at the giant fan revolving above us. It resembled the propeller of a plane. Maybe it was one.

"Please come in and relax, Seymour, let me get you a cold drink. You have worked overtime for me and gone out of your way and I wish to express my deepest appreciation."

Was this dude for real? I handed him the two packages, speechless and confused. He seemed so genuine, intimately polite, a true gentleman. But how could that be? I'd pictured an evil monster, yet here he was, Mr Niceness.

He motioned me to a seat in a room full of white satin couches and glass-fronted cabinets, the latter home to many colorful curios. Without waiting for my response to his query about liquid libations, he went behind the well-stocked wet bar and poured us a couple of icy drinks.

I sipped mine: a sweetish concoction with fresh mint and a hint of lime. It had alcohol in it too, a potent tequila, but not much. Enough, however, that I began to relax.

After sitting down on the couch across from me, my host opened the jewelry box and removed the pendant, holding it up to admire the handiwork. "Beautiful," he said, his black eyes shining with what I think were tears. "He does such a marvelous job, does he not?" he asked rhetorically.

I felt kind of sorry for the guy. Yes, his business was causing serious problems for the environment and for Florida citizens, as well as health issues for many Americans, but he was a human being and his wife had just died. I kept silent, swallowing my resentment with gulps of the cold drink.

He got up and walked over to one of the glass cabinets. When he opened it I could see it was a kind of showcase for pendants. I counted nine of them, each hanging by a silver chain against a backdrop of white satin. Some of the pendants were shaped like hearts, others like birds or fish. I spied a mermaid, a baseball or softball, a cat, a butterfly.

What the *hell*? How many wives had the man had – and lost? Did he have their heads chopped off when they displeased him?

My mouth must have been hanging open because after closing the cabinet he turned around again and smiled reassuringly at me. "I've had bad luck with my bitches. I seem to fall for the ones with serious physical weaknesses."

I stood up. Walking quickly to the wet bar, I set down my empty tumbler. I thanked him for his hospitality. Then I rushed out of the room, mumbling nonsense about how I was due back in Hollywood and needed to see to my car.

He followed me out to the vestibule, flustered and apologetic.

Without explanation, I turned down his offer of a limo ride to my car. Then I fled.

It took me less than ten minutes to jog to the bridge. When I arrived at my car the hood was down and the engine was running. Purring, actually.

Chester was seated in the driver's seat. He smiled up at me. "She's fine. Timing belt. But you should buy only the good gasoline, okay?"

I gave him a twenty and drove him back to the estate. I ran him right up to the portico. Before I dropped him off he said, "Too bad about Mr F's dog. She was a nice girl, pretty golden retriever. You probably cheer him up. He been very sad all day."

When I arrived home I went straight to the liquor cabinet. Then I called Yvonne and told her the whole story. We both laughed so hard we were crying.

After we hung up, I ordered a large pizza with every kind of topping, then sat out on the patio with Catcher until the doorbell rang.

Unnecessary Sermons

I T WAS A dark, humid morning and when she called Yvonne sounded especially glum. The Manahans had left her alone, but she was still afraid of what they might do. She hadn't tried to find a new position and was running through her savings. She knew it was time to move on but she felt stuck, still paralyzed with grief.

I knew the feeling. And I knew something that might help. Temporarily.

Outside, black storm clouds pounded on the flat gray sky like hammers on anvils. It was a perfect day for a funeral.

So when our phone conversation paused, I invited Yvonne to join me on a grief gig.

She had to have been desperate: because she agreed to meet me at noon at the Mer de l'Eau Chapel.

A funeral date. How romantic.

After we hung up I wandered into the kitchen and stared at my home bar. I allowed my blurry eyes to caress the selection lining the long oak shelf. Prescription muscle relaxants, antidepressants, over-the-counter pain pills. Behind the row of pill bottles, bigger bottles in an enticing mix of colors and shapes. Expensive distilled liquors. Cheap whiskey for the quick morning-after shot in a cup of hot coffee. Fancy after-dinner brandies. An expensive bottle of burgundy that should've been kept in a wine cellar.

It took everything I had and a little more to turn away and head for the shower. By the time I'd made myself presentable and donned my funeral uniform I had just enough time to make it to the chapel.

One lousy day at a time.

The parking lot was bereft of cars. The chapel, a thin pine structure built in the 1950s which appeared to be rotting where it stood, was nearly empty. The funeral procession consisted almost entirely of professionals in black suits and matching masks. Six funeral home employees were present, together with a reverend dressed in lay clothing and a bad toupee and an elderly woman with thick glasses who was being paid by the hour to play the organ. The real mourners sat up front, three people spread out across the pews.

I wondered why Raymond had failed to recruit more freelancers for the job. To see so few people at a final ceremony made me cringe for her.

Her being the deceased. A former Hollywood legend and household name. Hollywood, California, that is. This woman had been a major film star. In honor of her fine reputation, I have not named her here. But you would certainly know her name. Everyone does.

Or did. At one time, everyone did.

Then this.

Reverend Bob removed his mask and introduced himself to the five of us seated in the pews, then he began to speak. I must've been looking for a reason to weep: I felt the tears well up while listening to what I usually saw through, the anonymous memorial tribute rich in pointless bathos. Beside me, Yvonne shed a steady stream of tears. Her emotions were for her own grief, as mine were for mine. I put my arm around her shoulder and we clung to one another in a kind of shared self-pity.

Occasional bursts of nearby thunder shook the chapel as Reverend Bob finished his well-rehearsed monologue. He stood there looking out at us, silent mourners breathing softly in the dankness. He asked if we wished to say something. Since the gathering was so intimate, he explained, he was opening the ceremony to all participants.

He rocked back on his heels and waited patiently, staring up at the unpainted ceiling with its scattered leaks. A hush settled over us.

A frail-looking elderly man in an expensive suit spoke up first. Upon removing his mask, his voice projected in a way that indicated he'd spent time on a stage. "Tween was my childhood friend. I've always loved her. Her parents took me into their home whenever I had family trouble, so she was like a sister to me. I knew she was going places even then, when the two of us were just kids. And back then I was her biggest fan. But oh, she had her faults." He smiled and looked to the other two mourners for confirmation. "At one point in our lives we argued horribly. For years after that we remained out of touch. But I cared for my dear friend. Tween was a gifted person. A special person. I only wish her fame and fortune had made her happier."

He bowed his bald head.

There was a younger man in the adjoining pew, dressed exquisitely in a tailored suit. Dark, lean, movie star handsome, he spoke next. "My mother was a commanding presence wherever she was, on screen or at home."

His voice was instantly familiar. Tween's well-known actor son! Yvonne smiled at me. She recognized him as well.

The son continued, his voice strong and full of emotion. "Those of us close to her understand only too well why there are but a handful of us here today."

There was so much pain in his face that his perfect features were distorted. I reminded myself he did this for a living, but I got chills just the same. When the son turned to stare at Yvonne and me, his expression was challenging, or maybe it was just plain curious.

Yvonne shrank against me and I nodded my head gravely while trying to muster a degree of dignity. This proved difficult: I was embarrassed to be an obvious interloper, plus Yvonne's warmth beside me was reminding me of something; her lithe body fit so perfectly under my arm.

Like Marnie.

Marnie with the red dress over her head, her pale skin glistening.

I dropped my arm and Yvonne stepped away. Instantly, I missed her touch.

The third mourner sat at the far end of the front pew. She spoke out of a shroud of black gauze. Her veiled hat resembled a bee-keeper's helmet, and her shaking voice reached us through a thick swathe of netting and mask. "My sister lived in her own world. She lived in a world where words hurt, where wounds never heal, where life experiences don't turn out for the best. In a bad luck world like that, you have a hard time hanging on to your friends and loved ones. You have a hard time hanging on to yourself. How am I going to mourn my sister's suicide when all I feel is gratitude? I'm just so glad she's not suffering anymore. And I'm glad *we* aren't either."

A long, uncomfortable silence followed.

I realized they were waiting for me to say something.

Shit.

My heart sped up. What could I say? Everyone was bitching about the deceased. Weren't we supposed to speak well of the dead, especially those whose corpses were barely cold? How could I say something sincere, something positive, when I'd never met the woman? She sounded like a person nobody could speak highly of. If I trotted out my usual lines on this occasion, wouldn't everyone know I was fabricating?

Of course they would.

Reverend Bob cleared his throat. Actor son's eyes bored holes in mine.

Uh oh.

I opened my mouth, unsure about what would come out.

"Sometimes the most difficult people to live without are the ones we found most difficult to live with." Yvonne was standing tall, her mask dangling from one ear, and she was speaking with the kind of confidence an attorney uses in closing arguments.

The old lady tilted her head to one side. She looked like she was willing to listen.

Encouraged, Yvonne continued. "Maybe you were angry or no longer on speaking terms, but when you hear that this individual who had an impact on your life . . . a big impact, maybe not always positive but an impact you could never deny, even to yourself . . . when you feel it for a fact when this person has left this earth, when you realize you'll never see their face again, it does something to you. It does something to your heart. Your heart lurches, it aches, and it races. It races *wildly*."

Yvonne lifted her hands to her chest, where her heart probably *was* racing. Mine was.

The chapel held its breath. Everyone was standing absolutely still. When a flock of parrots flew overhead, squawking loudly from above the leaky roof, we all flinched.

Except Yvonne. She kept speaking. "No one ever warned me about this kind of grief. Nobody tells you how it feels so much like fear. I'm not afraid, not really, but the sensation is a lot like being scared. I'm on high alert and I don't even know why. I feel like I have a mild concussion. I'm walking around in a daze but with my adrenaline on the edge of spiking. Twenty-four seven." She held up her hand and let the trembling show. "And underneath this strange and debilitating emotional state lies so much sadness. The weird, futile sadness that is grief."

I grabbed her hand and moored us down.

She gripped my hand tightly. "The insurmountable grief that comes with knowing that this person is no longer in your life. The hurt is gone, replaced by a new kind of hurt. Because now you can never love them right, and they can never love you right either. It's too late to make things right between you."

Her face was streaked with tears. It looked like she'd wrung a few tears out of the three bereaved as well. They wiped their eyes before turning around to the minister again.

Reverend Bob nodded his head at us. As if to say, *Good job.*

I was impressed. Yvonne had talent. She could easily find work as a professional griever.

Reverend Bob talked for a few minutes, then led the scanty bunch of real mourners out front. They stood together by the limousine. Yvonne and I stayed back, standing together under the entryway awning.

The heavy rain had diminished to a fine misting and the sun was attempting to cook the excess water out of the sodden and shining world around us. The beach was so close I could hear the tidal suck. The sky was yellowish, sallow-looking, but the air smelled recently dry-cleaned.

We watched as the funeral home employees hoisted the dusky rose casket and slid it into the yawning mouth of the hearse.

"Are we going to the cemetery? Or can we go get a cup of coffee instead?" Yvonne asked me.

"If we stick around, we might have to field questions we don't want to answer," I responded. "Usually at these gigs I'm just a guy in a dark suit in the crowd and nobody notices me." I took out my phone. "I'll notify my employer, then we can go."

After I had left a message on Raymond's voicemail about my decision not to risk exposure at the burial site, I offered to drive us to La Cantina.

Yvonne wanted to walk to the beach instead. "Let's take the boardwalk. Then we can sit somewhere quiet. I feel wrung out."

The choice to walk was an excellent one. The boardwalk was deserted because of the inclement weather, but the dark clouds were drifting away. As we walked, the sky gradually brightened and the beach began to fill up. Sun worshippers in skimpy bathing suits, running children, lovers holding hands, and families with baskets of food and coolers of cold drinks.

I was dripping sweat by the time we found a hotel veranda and ducked out of the noon sun's full-on glare. I pointed to a wicker couch under a rattan paddle fan, and Yvonne sat down. She fanned herself with her hands. The air was clammy, the desultory breeze mildly helpful.

When I asked if she'd prefer the air-conditioned lobby, she shook her head. "The view from here is perfect," she said.

And it was. Turquoise sea, white sand, people enjoying themselves on a beautiful day.

When a hotel employee in a flowery shirt offered us frosted glasses of key limeade, we readily accepted. Tourists flip-flopped out of the hotel, passing by us on their way to the beach. Royal terns and black-headed laughing gulls hovered above the small dunes. Everything felt salty and sticky, full of life. Normal life, like when there was no killer virus and death was not circling around all of us.

Yvonne drained her drink. "That minister was great. Allowing everyone to speak about their feelings was a really good idea."

Her face was pink from the heat. She looked less like a white rose and more like a lovely woman. She was *such* a lovely woman.

"I was impressed by *your* speech," I told her. "People are typically ashamed of their anger with the person who died. They don't know what to expect, and they can't explain their grief. They're confused. You were able to summarize the effects of these complex emotions. I think your words had a good effect on the bereaved."

"And nobody took out a handgun, so that was a pleasant change," she joked. "But in general, this one was the same as Bill's ceremony. Relatively few people paying their respects to a person almost nobody is actually mourning. Some days I feel like

I'm the only one who cares that he died." She sighed. "And I *am* angry with Bill, I really am. I've got all sorts of mixed emotions. I hate him for leaving me. I wish he'd run off with me when we had a chance. I blame him for being so stupid that he thought he could actually tell them he quit. You can't just up and leave when you want to! He basically committed suicide, like the bitch whose funeral we just attended. No thoughts about those they're leaving behind. How *we'll* feel. What will happen to *us*."

She sighed again, then rested her head against my arm where I'd stretched it across the back of the couch. Her hair was russet in the light. Delicate strands spread along my shirt sleeve. I knew I would be taking some home with me.

Eyes closed, she said, "I don't know how you can attend these events all the time. Doesn't it depress you to face the loved ones of deceased individuals so miserably unpopular you've been hired to fill out the funeral roster? I mean, wouldn't it be more life-affirming to attend big end-of-life celebrations? Where lots of people remember an important life, a valued person? Rather than a handful of haters who struggle to say something about someone nobody liked?"

I knew what she meant but I didn't agree. Maybe I once thought that way, but not anymore. I knew too much about death and the grief that went with it.

I said, "Before I started this job I could barely motivate myself to sit at a table and focus on a crossword puzzle. I ate little, drank too much, and spoke mainly to a feral cat who comes to my backyard for handouts. When I looked in the mirror I saw a con-temptible old man, a person who would've been better off dead. In fact, I was the *walking dead*, headed for a funeral nobody would attend. I barely qualified as a living being anymore, I was almost a *nonbeing*. That kind of existence? It's like a form of suicide. Slow suicide."

A large gull landed on the sidewalk in front of us. It pecked at an invisible delectable before flying off. In the distance, a deeply tanned man with a purple beach umbrella on his shoulder was making his way slowly across the hilly sand.

I said, "Now I've found a crumb of meaning in my small mouthful of a life. I feel like I can make the tiniest difference in the lives of a few individuals. I'm helping to preserve the dignity of the forgotten or unloved. When I promise a client one warm body in a pew or at a gravesite, I think maybe it makes their death easier." I shrugged. "I don't know, perhaps I'm wrong and I'm merely enabling their self-delusions. Perhaps they're only using me to comfort themselves by buying whatever they think they need. This may be exactly what created their unpopularity in the first place. I've thought about all that, and I'm not sure what the psychologists would say. But I do know this: granting these people their dying wish has helped me feel more alive. I haven't actually moved on from my own loss, but at least I'm no longer in a zombie coma. I'm not the walking dead anymore."

Yvonne's eyes were still closed; we were both quiet for a while. The tide was going out. I could barely hear the crash of it anymore. The easterly wind had died but I could still smell the briny odor of distant sea-beds.

We breathed in sync in the calming sea air.

When Yvonne opened her eyes she looked tired, wrung out like she'd said earlier. "I don't want to enlist in the army of bitter, wronged women. No point in that. I hope when I get further along in my grieving process, I'll figure out something worthwhile to do with my life. If the Manahans don't have me killed first, that is."

I tightened my arm around her shoulder and hugged her to me. I hoped she was speaking out of ignorance and fear, but what did I know? Ignorant and fearful myself, there was nothing I could say.

We watched the old man with the purple umbrella as he

dragged it along the sidewalk behind him. He carefully mounted the wooden steps to the veranda, one hobbled foot at a time, the umbrella bumping up the stairs behind him. I marveled at the human engine, how it goes and goes. How it always wears out eventually.

When he reached the couch, the old man stopped to stare at us. Wrinkled and coffee-stain brown, he resembled a sun-kissed raisin. He winked at me. "Nice piece 'a pie you got there, buddy."

After he disappeared inside the lobby, Yvonne lurched forward to let out a booming laugh.

We sat there laughing for quite some time.

Dream Interlude I

I'M STANDING IN front of a classroom of students. There's no heat and the room is cold, freezing cold. It's loud, the clamor, the kids unruly and out of control. Most of the students are ignoring me, romping around and yelling nonsense at one another. A group of teenage boys in the back are huddled around a cell phone, sniggering ominously. I'm in charge, supposedly, but no one is listening to me.

Two girls seated in the front row have their hands over their mouths, their narrow shoulders shaking with laughter. They seem to be laughing at *me*.

I try to stare them down but I realize one is Marnie, the other Yvonne.

Marnie is dressed in a navy-blue no-nonsense suit, something the real Marnie would never wear. Her eyes sparkle. Yvonne's tight jeans and candy-striped tube top make her look like she's fourteen or fifteen, and her rusty hair shines in thick plaits that almost touch her waist. She's wearing a black leather shoulder holster with a 9 mm Beretta tucked inside. A clunky army gun.

I'm trying to get the class to quiet down but they won't listen. So I'm feeling humiliated, yet weirdly excited. Turned on. I'm sure I'll be fired from my job, but I can do nothing to change the situation. I'm helpless before these rowdy boys. These beautiful girls.

I continue to stand there, not in control. I'm not in control of the class. I'm not in control of my life.

Before the chaos in front of me erupted, I'd been lecturing about feeling tone in the classic post-postmodern novel. They were bored so their attention wandered, and suddenly it was an absolute zoo.

Without knowing why, I blurt out, "Misery loves a crowd."

Yvonne and Marnie snicker. Nobody else notices – or cares.

Mr Untouchable appears in the front row wearing a red and white striped beach robe that falls to his knees. His skin is evenly browned, his face chiseled stone. "Did I ever tell you about my art collection?" he says to Marnie.

He hands her a black jewelry box and she pops it open. Her eyes widen as she stares at a dusty blue pendant.

Her ashes are forever, I think.

Mr Untouchable boasts, "Masterpieces, babe. Matisse, Monet, you name it. Wyeth, Warhol. Gorgeous, right? But see, they're all fakes. My guys, they can make fakes so good you gotta believe in them. You believe in them! Just like these knockoff Cartier cuffs."

He holds out a set of shiny gold handcuffs. Marnie arranges one cuff on her narrow wrist, allowing him to snap it in place. He's grinning now, basking in the glow from her adoring eyes. He fits the other cuff to his own wrist and closes the clasp with a brisk click. Then he leans in and they kiss.

I watch like they're on late night television. Half there, half asleep, my mind keeps repeating a singular phrase: *plausible deniability.*

Yvonne raises her hand. She hasn't shaved her underarms and the hair is curly, auburn. She smiles, revealing the braces on her teeth. She's young enough to be my granddaughter. I try to look away but my eyes seek out her body again. I'm intensely attracted to her.

What a depraved piece of shit I am. An everyday asshole, only worse. Worse than my own father, even.

Yvonne smacks her gum. Blows a bubble that grows larger and larger until it pops. "What if mañana never comes, Mr Allan?" she asks in a loud voice.

Suddenly, the class falls silent.

Dead silent.

Death by Water Trade

AFTER THAT, THE grief work dried up. I called Raymond almost every day, but he always said he was sorry, he had nothing for me. Snowbirds were back up north, older folks weren't going out, the latest virus spike had settled down. Late summer doldrums, Raymond claimed. The dog days in Florida.

Without work, each day was like the preceding days, only more so. The heat pushed down on my skull like a fat hangover headache. My actual hangover headaches beat on my head like a sun hammer until I couldn't stand them anymore. I sat out on the patio, crippled by my own malaise. I often found myself wishing for the distraction of a crisis. A death, a shootout, a dead body to bury, a threat to my own sorry life. Anything but the nothing that was my everyday existence in a retirement village in Florida.

But I had no such luck. In fact, nothing happened for days, then weeks. Then the long weeks turned into months. Meanwhile, the sun pounded down, the palm trees swayed in sea breezes, the grass turned brown then green again after the heavy rains came down. Ixora blooms speckled the view in Crayola reds and yellows, frangipani blossoms exuded their sweet perfume. Great blue herons flew by, occasionally dropping down to stalk something on the outer edges of my yard. Iguanas bred and pooped and my neighbors chased them, clubbing them with broom handles.

I stared at crossword puzzles while the dregs of my coffee turned cold.

The sense of infinite sameness and the torturous feeling of waiting for something, anything, anything other than what I was experiencing, was intolerable. Yet I continued to live. I continued to tolerate my uselessness and my endless suffering.

When fall arrived, you wouldn't have known it. The hot humid days were a bit shorter, but just as insufferable.

One lazy afternoon in late September I was dozing in my usual seat out on the patio. Between naps, I twiddled my thumbs until the action created a mini-breeze. The sky was a boring blue, a perfect empty blue. My boy Catcher wasn't around, Yvonne had been distant lately, and there I was, alone with a cup of home-brewed coffee. As aimless as a man could be.

A four-foot-long neon-orange iguana made his way slowly across the lawn toward the narrow canal between my lot and my back neighbor's. The creature crept forward with a sinuous grace. Suddenly, its spiny head burst open. Iguana brain and skin scattered across the bright green grass.

My back neighbor, an eighty-year-old former book publicist, approached the carcass, air rifle at his side. When he spotted me in my screenless patio he flashed me the V for victory sign.

The South Florida version of a strict anti-immigration policy. Iguanas were not native, they were intruders, so we were to kill these immigrants before they ruined our country.

Disgusted, I retreated inside. I ignored the beckoning home bar and called Raymond from the landline in the kitchen.

He answered on the first ring. "Seymour! Looking for work? Because I may have something for you. *If* you can be open minded about it."

Open minded? That could only mean one thing. "Boca," I said with a lump in my throat.

"Yes. It's his time."

Raymond knew I'd take the job. He knew I needed the cash, he knew I thrived on the social interaction and stimulation his free-lance assignments provided. He understood this about me, which was why he'd been able to recruit me so easily. And now that I'd been in he knew I didn't want out. I couldn't stand being out. He knew this too.

He took a scolding tone with me. "So you're willing to go up to Boca again? Complete the bedside grief case? Do it *right* this time by spending quality *end* time with the client?"

He waited for me to confirm. He wanted me to admit to both of us that I'd rather risk what was left of my life than not have a life at all.

I took a deep breath, exhaling slowly. The lumbering refriger-ator claiming most of the space in my galley kitchen hummed, vibrating loudly on the tile floor. Amtrak was speeding through town a quarter-mile to the east, on its way north from Miami. The horn blared as it reached a crossing.

Raymond remained silent, patient with me until I was able to gather my thoughts into a neat sentence or two. Which I finally did.

"A good death is nothing to fear," I told him. "It's important we help the dying avoid a lack of faith, a sense of despair, spiritual pride, or last-minute greed. Milton Lasker could use guidance in these areas during his final days."

A tight little speech. Cribbed from the indoctrination provided by Professional Grievers, Inc.

"Very nice, Seymour. I see you've been reading the little book I sent you." I imagined the shallow smile on Raymond's pale face, the twist of his narrow lips. "Every American should take the time to read *Ars Moriendi*. The culture needs to change. We must all learn to see there is a distinctive upside to death."

Easy for him to say. He wasn't on his deathbed. Yet. What would he say then?

But I only sighed in vague agreement. I needed the money. And I ached for something meaningful to do.

"Okay, Seymour, I'm glad you are willing to return to your unfinished case. Now, I must warn you that Mr Lasker has changed since you last saw him. He's gone downhill. When he became gravely ill again, he demanded emergency surgery. This was not recommended, as you may recall. But he found a surgeon who complied with his demands. Of course, there was nothing the doctor could do. It was too late."

Stubborn bastard. I felt no pity for the man.

"The procedure and the hospitalization that followed have drained him of energy and he's lost the will to live. At this point, he is confined to his bed at home. He has asked that you spend his final days with him, that you forgive him and come to his bedside. He told me to tell you that he does not expect an infusion of life force and positivity this time. Only a friend by his side."

A *friend*? What kind of friend do you choke and dump? No infusions would be coming from me. In fact, I was relieved to hear he was weakened. Still, I planned to keep my distance. I rubbed my throat. It hurt just thinking about Lasker's steely hands.

"May I notify Mr Lasker you'll be arriving tonight?" Raymond asked, then hung up before I could answer. Apparently, this had been a rhetorical question, a demand disguised as a query.

Fine. I'd pack and go. Back to fucking Boca Raton.

As I hung up the phone, I wondered if Lasker had been paying Raymond to shut me out, or whether Raymond had decided on his own to stop assigning me grief cases in order to lure me back to Boca. Either way, I felt cheap. Used and manipulated. But, I realized, I was also vastly relieved. Relieved to have the work. Money coming in, and a place to go. Somewhere to be outside my own interior prison, my own boring head.

I hadn't had a drink for twenty-six days. More than three weeks without the blanket pulled over my eyes, without the soothing blackness in which to rest my weary mind. I'd quit after Yvonne refused to talk to me one night. I'd been blubbering drunkenly, I guess, before she stopped me. All she said was, "I lost one close friend this year already. I'm not going to stand by while another makes his way into an early grave."

The sound of the dial tone after she hung up pierced my heart. Something clicked in my brain, despite the thick alcohol slush I'd cushioned it with.

I began spending more time at La Cantina, sipping cold coffee and staring blindly at stupid crossword puzzles. At night I sat out back on the patio. But *sans* the booze.

Boca wouldn't be a problem alcohol wise. I doubted Milton Lasker would be serving drinks. Not in his current state.

With a mild feeling of positivity, I got ready for another foray into the heart of dangerous luxury. It sure beat hanging around the retirement village, even if Boca and Mr Lasker made my blood pressure soar. Yes, I'd be under threat. And I would have to tolerate being back in that city, that horrible lovely elitist limbo. But duty – and money, and a deep need for emotional connection – called.

My packed duffel bag was still sitting in a heap in a dusty corner of my bedroom, where I'd tossed it after stumbling home from the park last spring. I pulled out Mr Lasker's gift clothes and did some laundry. I would use the outfits he'd bought me, wear them like a uniform. I would don the costume, play the role. Bedside griever, friend at the end. The night in the park, his hands around my neck, the autistic bodyguard, it all seemed like a bad dream now.

A nightmare I hoped I wouldn't be having again.

I went to my bookshelf and skimmed through the titles, selecting a handful of books to bring with me. Nothing inspirational, mostly dull classics, literature to sleep to. Then I brewed a pot of coffee and opened a can of tuna for Catcher. I set the can on the floor of the patio and waited for him to appear. While I drank three cups of coffee, prepping my system for all-night vigils, I watched the sun set in the distance.

Catcher didn't show.

The drive north on I-95 was unpleasant, as always. Kamikaze motorcycles passed me on the right at a hundred miles an hour. Menacing SUVs crowded my bumper, then whooshed past while kids gave me the finger from the back window. My Toyota was not doing so well. The rear end had come loose and the car shook violently now if I went over sixty. I had to be content with taking my time in transit. And taking shit from other drivers.

The radio station played Black Sabbath and KISS. I tried to remember what Marnie's favorite band was. Green something? I couldn't recall. I vaguely recalled her playing Motown music. And some of the newer girl groups. But I wasn't sure anymore. Yvonne was a huge fan of Nirvana. I could see that. I'd been developing a liking for them. Their songs had enough edge that they spoke to the raw part of me, the bleeding part. I could relate to the suicidal underpinnings.

When I pulled off the highway and drove east on Palmetto Park Road all the trees seemed bigger, more lush. The farther east I traveled, the richer the landscape around me became. Giant Royal Poinciana trees dripping bright orange flowers canopied the streets. Vivid yellow and purple blossoms from Golden Trumpet and Hong Kong Orchids added to the blaze of color I was passing through. Hundreds of regal palms towered over the road.

Approaching the bridge to the beach, I passed the pastel pink and green mansions that lined the road. I drove past mansion after mansion after construction site for new mansion after mansion.

My heart sped up, adrenaline zinging through my bloodstream. I was out of my element, way out of my league. Boca was a real stretch for a guy like me. And I didn't like to stretch. I especially didn't like to stick my neck out where it had been previously grabbed and throttled.

And then I was there, at Milton Lasker's. To my surprise, the driveway was rutted, the sea grape trees so full they blocked the view of the house. The place looked unkempt. Had he fired the gardener? Let go the help?

By the time I parked the car by the garage, my pulse was pounding in my head. My body was behaving as if my life was in danger. Would I be all alone with Lasker? Did he want me there so *he* could finish the job?

I put my head down on the steering wheel. I kind of prayed. I wasn't much for petitioning the Lord, but I asked for help. Please, I begged, don't let me walk into a trap. It would be too humiliating to get killed by a dying man.

I thought my prayers had been answered when my door suddenly swung open. An angel, here to help me through this dangerous time!

But it was only Vigo. He wore a mask so I put mine on too.

I climbed out of the car and looked up at him. His typically inert face registered something that resembled emotion. He reached for me and I flinched.

Uh oh, here it comes.

Vigo wrapped his powerful arms around me. He hugged me to his wide, muscular chest. His clutch was gentle, not deadly, and he was making a faint, repetitive sound. I stood there frozen in fear.

It took me a minute to realize he was whimpering. The big guy was either grief-stricken or scared. Maybe both.

I patted his back, wondering if he could hear the rapid knock-knock of my heartbeat.

After a while he let go of me and opened the back door to retrieve my bag. Then he led the way. I followed him through the white on white marble foyer into the great room. A hospital bed had been set up on the Persian rug in front of the giant fireplace I'd thought was only for show. After all, when would one need to light up the hearth in the year-round heat of South Florida?

Apparently, I'd been wrong. The majestic fireplace was in use. A raging fire had heated up the room. It felt like a hundred degrees in there. Sweltering, unbearable.

I stood there, adjusting. Then I stepped closer to the fire and the hospital bed.

The body in the bed looked completely alien. Milton Lasker was gone, and in his place a yellow skeleton had appeared.

Vigo took off with my duffel bag, most likely to the pool house where I'd stayed on my previous visit.

Taking measured steps across the thick rug, I reached the bed. Mr Lasker's deathbed. I sucked in my breath.

A small bald head rested on a pile of crisp white pillows. The skin was butter-colored, with the grainy texture of a headstone. The body between the tight white sheets was so small and flat it barely wrinkled them. Mr Lasker now resembled the pyred corpse of a hundred-year-old Indian beggar.

Still, I was scared. My legs felt like jelly. This was the man who'd almost killed me.

He opened his eyes. "Seymour," he croaked.

I jumped.

He flashed a Halloween smile, all bones and teeth.

My lips quivered but I was unable to manage a smile. He smelled like cider. Fermentation and rot.

When he reached for my hand, the movement was surprisingly quick. His fingers were dry and warm. It was like holding hands with a piece of toast.

I held my breath and allowed him to hang on.

We stared at one another. I could see something in his face. Resignation, relief. The keen intelligence was still there, but the rage was gone. So were the other attributes I'd thought of as central to Mr Lasker's character. Like the testosterone-driven strength, the ballsy verve that once drew me to this complicated man. The room, the bed, the man were empty of all that.

Mr Lasker had emptied himself of himself.

"Did you bring me some poetry, Seymour?" he whispered.

When I nodded, his dark eyes lit up. He let go of my hand and pushed himself to a sitting position. The sheet slid down a bit, revealing his concave belly. His chest was so thin I could count the ribs. So many ribs!

I helped him prop himself against the pillows and resettle the sheet. He felt as light as a tray of brownies.

I dragged over my favorite embroidered chair with a high back and padded arms, setting it next to the bed. I'd done this before, sat next to him while he was bedridden. But we were different this time, Mr Lasker and I. This time we would get it done. Do the work. Finish the case.

"Let's talk for a minute," I said. "Then we can read poetry. We can do whatever you want."

He said nothing. I gazed in his eyes, which were bloodshot and rimmed with shadows.

In a calm voice that belied my fear, I said, "I need to know why you almost killed me that day. I need to know what would make you want me dead."

It's unnerving to feel on you the beady eyes of an almost dead man, a scary scarecrow death stare that bores into you like lasers from the beyond. It's even more unsettling to face a person who once tried to kill you, but who has become so debilitated you could snuff out their life as easily as picking off a slow-moving iguana with a BB gun.

This thought was oddly amusing. I pictured myself aiming an air gun at his Brazil nut skull. *Poof.* Brains and skin everywhere.

A thick log shifted in the hearth and sparks flew. The room was like a sauna. Sweat dripped on to my upper lip, trailed down the sides of my face. The back of my shirt was soaked. If he lingered for more than a day or two I would be losing weight.

The death diet. The deathbed diet. Not a bad marketing concept. If I'd been a different sort of person, a more brazen business-minded person, maybe I could've capitalized on the experience. These days, people seemed to be able to capitalize on almost any experience.

"Seymour, my friend, I didn't try to kill you. If I'd wanted to kill you, I would've. And I wouldn't have left you lying in a public place."

I could see that. I started to speak but he held up a withered hand.

In a stronger voice, he said, "I acted out of hurt and anger about what I'd been led to believe was mislaid trust. Please, you gotta forgive me my mistake. I feel awful I caused you pain." He pointed a twiggy finger at me. "They told me false information so I'd get rid of you. Somebody wants you outta the picture. That's what that was all about."

A cold shudder iced through my sweat, chilling me. *Somebody wants you outta the picture.*

He spoke slowly, with what looked like great difficulty. "Maybe I can help you, Seymour. Let me make it up to you. I can find out what their beef is with you and take care of it."

His voice had a kind of energy when he said this. He shifted his tinker-toy limbs, his hard eyes on mine. The idea of assisting me was giving him strength. He wanted to do something, to be of service before reality set in and he couldn't do anything. Ever again.

I understood his position.

I sat back in the chair, thinking. So it wasn't what Raymond had told him that triggered Lasker's violent attack on me. What was it, then? The fire and his attitude were melting the icicles of fear in my veins, but my mind continued to wrestle with itself. *Be wary of this guy; don't be a pussy, he's made of straw. Confide in this man, he can help you; don't speak about your past, especially to this unpredictable criminal.*

He interrupted my internal debate. "Look, I'm gonna level with you here. Because I'm on my way out I'll tell you some things I woulda never told you otherwise. Then you can decide whether or not to trust me. Okay?"

He sat up a little straighter and his baggy eyes showed a glint of their old sparkle. The fire behind him made the whites of his eyes look redder than they were. Sparkling red eyes, the eyes of a vulture. He was circling his own dead body.

He said, "I told you I was in the publishing business in New York, and I was. But there's more to my work story. See . . ."

Vigo appeared with a blue plastic sippy cup. The kind you use with toddlers. Mr Lasker suckled the tiny straw while Vigo held the cup.

Watching this depressed me. Death was so humiliating, so damn humbling.

When he'd had enough, Mr Lasker pushed the cup away. "Stay, Vigo," he said, as if to a dog.

Vigo stood beside me, still holding the child's plastic cup. His close bulk made me feel even hotter and my body streamed with sweat under my clothes. I mopped my forehead with my handkerchief. The mask was making me feel even hotter, but I kept it on to protect Mr Lasker.

How ridiculous.

"Once you have money there are so many ways to make more money," he stated, his ravaged eyes on mine. "Ways that cut through red tape, ways that cross boundaries and skip steps and ease by regulations and restrictions. I don't want to go into all the ways I found to enhance my income, but believe me, I had a talent for it. Making money had always been pleasurable for me, but the illicit money brought me an inexplicable joy. It was better than a great game of golf. Better than sex with a goddess. Nothing compared to the big score. I loved raking it in. I was a fucking addict willing to do whatever it took. This included accepting the company I hadda keep in order to play in the big game. I made my own mountaintop, Seymour, don't get me wrong. But up there at the top? I had to play with all the other dirty players. You know what I'm saying?"

Oh, I knew what he was saying, all right. Sell out, get rich, feel like a winner, then die alone. I'd been observing this exact phenomenon since becoming a professional griever. It made me think of the Sixth Rule of Professional Grievers: We must forget about the dividends. We invest in our own lives with the expectation of a good return in the future. On our deathbed, we need to let go of all such expectations. There is no future anymore and the amount of one's personal fortune becomes totally meaningless. Milton Lasker needed to grasp this concept. It was important.

I started to tell him this, but he turned away and began to cough. He coughed and coughed until he choked.

Vigo quickly left the room, returning with a glass pitcher. Cubes thunked against the sides as he poured ice water into the plastic cup. Then Vigo helped his boss drink through the straw again.

I looked around the room. No bottles of medications, no morphine drip, no piles of pill containers next to the bed. Mr Lasker was going out cold turkey. Just glasses of water, and the company of his so-called friends.

As if reading my mind, he cleared his throat and said, "I want to check out with all my faculties intact. My mind is clear right now, clear like it hasn't been for years and years. If I can, I wanna die with my mind as it is right this minute. If that's how it works – and I'm taking a gamble that it does."

"And the pain?" I asked. "What about the pain?"

"There's no physical pain," he said with a small smile. "Only the pain that comes from knowing you played the game to win when you shouldda played it another way. That's all that bothers me now. That's why I wanted you to come, Seymour. So I could maybe help you like you helped me when you were here the last time. You inspired me to do things I didn't think I could do anymore. You made me wanna live. To *really* live. You made me think. You made me rethink the meaning of my life."

Really? All I remembered doing was hanging around in uncomfortable clothes, taking the man's handouts and bitching to Raymond about having to stay on indefinitely in the ritzy country club atmosphere. In a city that spoke to me silently of all my failings, that reminded me so acutely of my own loser status. Of my own terrible loss.

I stared at my feet in their cheap loafers. I felt ashamed of my selfish behavior during my previous assignment. Lasker had found my presence more meaningful than I'd imagined. Maybe choking me until I passed out and offloading me in an empty park had served to help him reclarify his priorities. Stranger reversals have happened throughout history, bizarre turnarounds enacted on deathbeds all over the world.

He hocked a bit to clear the phlegm from his throat. "Seymour, what you need to understand is this. Once I became a wealthy man the people around me were there for one and only one reason. They wanted me to give them some of what I had. My fucking assets were what they wanted, not my friendship. Knowing this made me hateful, distrustful, until eventually I drove away everyone close to me. I'm a thoughtful man, Seymour, you know that about me. I may be immoral, sinful, but I know right from wrong and I know myself. I know what I've done to the people around me. That's why I'm alone on my deathbed for the second time. Except for Vigo, my faithful friend and employee. And you, Seymour."

Behind me, Vigo made the whimpering sound again. The noise was so alien and forlorn, so primitive and real, my eyes teared up.

"You are my friends, and I trust you two. Only you. Vigo has been with me since he was a kid. I love Vigo and he's been devoted to me."

I didn't dare look at Vigo.

"You, Seymour, I don't know why I love you, I just do. We connect on some soul level. Like brothers. I'm sorry I allowed myself to be misled about you. I know you would never fuck over the fucking Gambo family. After I hurt you that night, I dug around and I found out what they did to you. I'm sorry I listened to Bobby G, and I can't believe I even thought for a minute you were here for any other purpose than to service my needs."

Wait. Gambo? Bobby G? Was that a G for Gambo? And what the fuck?

I was stunned. I sat there struggling to put two and two together but my mind stalled.

Lasker coughed again until Vigo fed him more water. He sank back against the pillows. He looked all out. This was too much for him.

I asked if he needed me to leave so he could rest.

He raised one hand, the bones visible though the thin skin. He couldn't hurt me now. Yet he had overpowered me such a short time before. How quickly the human body diminished.

"No, no. Please, Seymour. I need to explain. I need to do this now, while I still can."

An antique grandfather clock announced the hour; a delicate tone lingered in the hot air after the eighth bell finished ringing. The feeling it gave me was spiritual, uplifting. Calming.

Mr Lasker said, "I want you to understand that I never joined any families or organized groups. I had no crew that reported to me for orders. I'm a Jew, an outsider. My publishing company gave me the capital to start with and introduced me to the people that could make my millions grow."

Good for you, I thought. But what good did it do him now?

"You know the kind of books I admire, Seymour, the respect I have for the written word. Without poetry, philosophy, art, we'd still be crawling around in the slime. But it's sex and grime that make the cut. The baser the better, as far as profits are concerned. And I was a businessman. So for decades I associated with men of massive means and minimal scruples. I met a lot of those guys over the years, we shared corporate war stories, had drinks. I knew what was what and who was what."

He paused to catch his breath. There are many ways to invest and seek dividends. Some are dirtier than others. It was no surprise to me that Mr Lasker had dirt on his hands from thumbing through sleazy magazines and shaking hands with smarmy publishers.

He continued. "I got to know people with ties to certain other people. And eventually I had enough dough to play with them. It seemed easy enough to join the big players at the biggest investment tables, so I launched a second career as a freelance financier. But the people I financed, that's where it got complicated. They were not always so legit. And the returns I got on my money, well, all those double- and triple-digit percentages were achieved by a variety of methods of questionable ethical and legal grounds."

He scowled, then waved it all away. "This doesn't make me unique, of course. And it hardly matters now. What matters to us at this moment is that I did some business over the years with the Gambo organization. This means I'm in a position to help someone like you. I'm friends of a sort with various family members who can say the word and your troubles will vanish. I would like to say the word for you, Seymour. I could die more comfortably if you would allow me to do this thing."

I swallowed hard. So Gambo meant Robert Gambo. Bobby, Bobby G. Mr Untouchable?

I must've looked confused because Mr Lasker chuckled. It

sounded like he'd swallowed a giant toad. "He doesn't know what I'm talking about, Vigo," he croaked.

Vigo placed a thick paw on my shoulder and kind of patted me. Hard. I flinched. His petting of me made me think about how I treated Catcher. I'd have to remember to be more gentle with that cat in the future.

"Seymour, Seymour. Do I have to spell it out for you? The woman you fell in love with, what happened to her? Let's start there and the rest will become clear to you."

He waited for me to figure it out. His eyes watched me. They were the eyes of a thousand-year-old man.

I listened to the old clock ticking away the time. Gone, gone, gone. None of us have much of it to waste, considering how fast it all slips away in the end.

I said, "Her name was Marnie and she ran a dance studio in town. I met her one night on the beach when I was out with my telescope. She seemed to enjoy my company and it didn't take long for me to fall for her. She was beautiful, intelligent. And young, so young I couldn't believe she'd sleep with me. I still don't know what she saw in me, but I was too crazy about her to question it. In the beginning, I mean. After a few months, that's all I did."

"She brought you down to the fucking cold dark place, you mean," Mr Lasker said, and I sighed in agreement. "All the beautiful ones do, Seymour. It's nothing to be ashamed of."

I shifted in my seat. Might as well spill it. Just let it all go. What could he do, turn me over to the Mob? Choke me again, tell Vigo to dump me on the beach? Whatever, I was tired of dragging myself around, guilty and burdened by my choices, my pathetic life.

So I told him everything.

"She warned me the first night that she had to be free to come and go. I said okay. Because I would've done anything, said anything, to be with her. And it was tolerable at first. As long as I could have her, what did the rest of her life matter? But soon enough it became unbearable. He'd call her and she'd go running. I couldn't say a thing. If I did, she left anyway and didn't come back for even longer. This made me mad with jealousy. I started drinking too much. Maybe her infidelity was just an excuse to drink, it certainly wasn't the only time I turned to alcohol. But she hated my drinking and we'd fight. I'm embarrassed to even talk about it. My behavior was so abysmal, I hardly recognized myself."

My voice choked off. Vigo rested a heavy hand on my shoulder, then left the room.

Mr Lasker raised his forehead where his eyebrows once were. "Go on, my friend."

Vigo returned with a glass for me. He filled it with ice water, which I downed in a single gulp. I thanked him, put my mask back in place, then said, "It got worse. I turned into a fucking snoop bastard. I followed her night after night until I'd pieced it all together. I had some training in investigation, you see. All those years as a high school teacher taught me to research the obvious until I found the backstory. We never talked about my teaching career, did we, Mr Lasker? It was always about you. What, you assumed I was born to grieve? I had a life before Professional Grievers, believe me."

He nodded, unblinking, accepting my reprimand. "I know you did. I looked into it, once you left here. I, too, can be a snoop bastard. When I care. Please continue," he said, a soft command.

No need to encourage me, I was unstoppable now, the story rolling out ahead of me like a dingy carpet to some distant end. "This man she would run off to see, he lives here. In west Boca on a five-acre estate in a fancy gated community."

Another reason to hate this fucking city. My main reason, in fact. Every time Marnie left me for him, she left me for fucking Boca Raton. She left me for Mr Untouchable. Why? Because

Mr Untouchable ran a private club for members only, an exclusive supper club that catered to men of extreme wealth. The top CEOs, kings of the Fortune 500, the mobster bosses, Wall Street wizards, sports stars and movie stars, these were the kind of men he invited to his club. Hand-engraved invitations were delivered by goons in tuxedos, the richest men in the country personally invited to drop in. To come on down. The word had been passed around for years, the club was legend, so everyone wanted to be included. To have the experience. It was a kind of status symbol, to spend the evening at Mr Untouchable's private supper club.

I took a deep breath. I could still hear the hum of the grandfather chime. It was stuck in my head along with everything else I would've rather not listened to.

"Marnie worked at the man's club. As a dancer. She worked whenever he called her in. He'd call and she'd hurry there to demean herself, to attend to the twisted whims of some celebrity visitor or wealthy regular." My voice was shaking now. With anger. With helplessness. "Marnie was indentured to this rich man with his elite sex club. And there was absolutely nothing I could do to change her situation. Nothing."

My voice faded. Vigo refilled my glass and I drank it down, drowning the humiliation and frustration that had taken away my words. My self-esteem. My sorry excuse for a life.

Mr Lasker stared at me with his tired doggy eyes. There was pity there as well as understanding. "I've been to that club, Seymour. I can imagine your pain. I'm no prude, I like a good whorehouse. But this club, the way the women are treated?" He shook his head, sympathetic to my despair.

I held up a hand. I didn't want to hear any details. I had enough guilt. I told him about the way I'd treated Marnie myself. On our final night together.

After that, we were quiet for a while. The fire shifted itself and the light in the room bounced around. The clock ticked away our pointless lives. I thought about how death might be a kind of welcome relief. Finally, all the pain would end.

I made a decision. I would tell the rest. The whole aching stab of it, the killer sadness, the deep wound truth, the end truth. I looked into Mr Lasker's black hole eyes and I stepped inside. As if from a comfortable, painless distance, I could hear my own voice. I sounded calm. Deathly calm.

"On her way up to Boca that same night, after I'd treated her so badly, Marnie was in a collision on I-95. A car swerved into her lane. Drunk driver. Marnie died instantly. The other driver was fine. Unscathed. A month later, however, he was found beaten to death in an alley in Hialeah. His murder remains unsolved."

I leapt up and paced the marble floor while Lasker struggled to subdue a fit of coughing. Maybe it was time for me to let the poor guy rest. I didn't want to push him closer to his final breath. Not anymore.

Had I forgiven him already?

When the coughing fit calmed down, he relaxed against the pillows and smiled at me. A ghoulish grin. "I can solve that mystery for you. The Gambo family operates the club, the one where your girlfriend worked. One of many operations they control here in South Florida. Bobby G runs the place. Manager. He must have had the driver of the car that hit your girlfriend, ah, *punished* for what he did. Because that drunken act, it took away from Bobby's business. Bobby doesn't like losing out on expected profits. He regards his girls as personal property, his beautiful means to an end. The end being ready access to millionaires and billionaires, politicians and celebrities, the world's biggest movers and shakers. Bobby G doesn't like to lose access. You couldn't have saved that poor girl, Seymour. There was no fucking way for you to help her." Mr Lasker sighed. "Wish I'd known. I could've put in a good word for her."

The tears streamed down my face. Vigo refreshed my drink and patted my shoulder again. Maybe he was more introspective than autistic. He could be comforting. A comforting presence.

"Perhaps you will let me intervene at this point," Mr Lasker said. "There's no reason for you to continue to suffer. You're sorry for your violent behavior with Marnie. You made a mistake and acted on your emotions, and the timing was indeed unfortunate. But the car accident was not your doing. Berating yourself for the rest of your life is not going to change what occurred by fate. It certainly wasn't your fault she was mixed up with Bobby G. What was she doing, working off a loan with a guy like that? Where was she from? So many of Bobby's girls come to the US from less fortunate places. They're hoping to model, and they end up working on their backs."

I was all too aware of this fact. I'd done my research. "Marnie wasn't an immigrant. She's from New Jersey. She had talent, but she couldn't make a living at dance so she took a job at a high-end strip club in Pompano. Dancing. One of the owners, it turns out, was Bobby G."

I imagined the confident young man in the society pages, his custom suits and his four-hundred-dollar haircuts. My body began to shake. My knees knocked together, so I steadied them with my trembling hands.

"Whenever he came into the strip club, he complimented Marnie on her dancing. He must've sensed the drive in her, her business sense, her charm with people. Because he offered to help her start up a dance studio. Which had always been her dream. So she was thrilled. Thrilled to get out of the strip club, thrilled to run her own business."

Her strip mall studio was lovely, the little girls in their pink tutus, the stay-at-home moms in their yoga gear, guys in jogging pants, everyone watching Marnie in the wall of mirrors as she demonstrated proper positions. I used to enjoy watching her too, dropping by when she completed a lesson, the students flocking around her, talking and laughing. They loved her.

I loved her.

I told Mr Lasker how I believed there were strings attached to the loan. How Bobby G must've called her on it, telling her his private club in Boca was the only way to pay off her debt. By the time I met Marnie she'd been running the dance studio for five years. I had no idea how long she'd been working at the sex club. She'd been conned and saw no way out of her situation. When we had the fight, the last one, she left me for that life. It had been killing both of us. But it killed her first.

When I finished my story Mr Lasker regarded me steadily while I recovered my composure. I mopped my face with my handkerchief.

The clock ticked on.

Coffee Spoons IV

A FEW DAYS BEFORE I went up to Boca to sit by Mr Lasker's bedside my neighbor died. Stella was eighty-something. She'd been an active, feisty, bright lady and I'd liked talking with her. But age had taken its toll. Her life had rapidly unspooled until she was spending her days slumped in a wheelchair, tended to by her Jamaican home health aide.

Both of the women liked Catcher, so when I hadn't seen him around for a while I'd go next door to talk to the girls.

The night Stella died I had dinner with them in Stella's immaculate kitchen. Chandice served us a spicy rice dish with red beans and a green chili sauce, along with baked chicken and pie. Ice cream pie from Publix.

"They make a mean pie," Stella said to me while Chandice fed her soupy spoonfuls of chocolate swirl. Catcher purred from Stella's tiny lap.

Stella had worked as a financial analyst on Wall Street and was the mother of two doctors, a pediatrician and an oncologist. Yet here she was in a diaper with near strangers, gumming baby food.

"You hear 'bout the iguanas?" Chandice wiped Stella's pale chin with a white linen napkin, then fed her another spoonful.

I shook my head. I hadn't been keeping up with local news.

"Village gonna pay someone to 'sterminate 'em." She shook her head without disturbing her tight ringlets.

Stella lifted a curled finger and pointed it at Chandice. "She's sad. She doesn't want the *poor things* to be poisoned." Chocolate bubbled on her wrinkled lips.

Chandice glanced at me before she stood up to clear the dessert plates. I arched my eyebrows as if to say, *I'm with you.*

But I wasn't. Not really. I wasn't aligned with either side on the subject. I didn't know what to think, or whether to even care. The iguanas on the loose in Emerald Day Village didn't bother me. I felt no need to shoot or poison them, chase or corner them. But neither did I want to save them all, carry a placard at city hall and plead for animal rights when the Village decided to rid the area of nuisance non-native animals.

"It's not the poor iguanas' fault they're running around, pooping on everybody's pool decks and eating their impatiens," Stella said, her eyes wide and lively. The room smelled like a hospital, a mix of ammonia and urine. "Green iguanas are an endangered species in Mexico. Poachers sell them to the dealers in Florida, they're the ones who let them go when they get too big to sell. So we're doing our civic duty, getting rid of invasives."

Chandice interjected, "Blow 'em up then, I don't care."

She had her back to us and the hot water running in the sink, but she turned fast when Stella made a loud farting noise with her mouth. Chocolate foam sprayed across the glass table and I jumped back, scraping my metal folding chair on the Mexican tile. Stella laughed when Catcher leaped from her lap. Her laugh was youthful, a girl's giggle. I had to smile.

"Chandice thinks the exotic animals have as much right to be here in Florida as us snowbirds. She thinks they're like immigrants," Stella said, her eyes full of a kind of prisoner's glee. "She thinks, what if the state decided to exterminate black folks?"

"Maybe they should 'sterminate old folks instead. You the ones costin' them so much money."

Stella laughed again. She was having fun bickering with Chandice.

I watched them banter, enjoying Stella's joy. The old woman's mouth was a horror of missing teeth. Her skull shone like an egg under the stark light of the fluorescent dome overhead. Slick white scalp peeked through her straggly purple-grey hair.

"What's your position on the iguana issue, Seymour?" she asked me.

I stood up and held out my hand to Stella. I grasped her knobby fist and held it steady. I had no idea, of course, that the last words I would ever say to my neighbor, except for thanking her for dinner and bidding her goodnight, would be this: "Is life all that sacred? I'm not so sure. It is, after all, just life."

Later that night the sirens woke me. I rolled over to go back to sleep. Which is what you do when you live in a retirement community, where ambulances arrive on a regular basis. There's always somebody falling down or having a coronary in Emerald Day Village. But when the pounding began at my front door I gave up on sleep. I crawled out of bed, wrapped myself in my raggedy robe, and shuffled out to the foyer.

As soon as I opened the door, Chandice fell against my chest. She smelled fetid, like bile and moldy blankets. Her unmalleable black curls were gone, the wig replaced by a harsh buzz cut. Chandice was a small woman, lean and wiry. I held her tight and let her listen to my steady heartbeat until she was able to control her weeping.

"We create our lives from one moment to the next," I said.

She sniffled and wiped her eyes, pulled away.

Stella's children shipped her body back to Scarsdale so that she could be buried in the family plot beside her husband and parents. Then they hired a realtor to list her house, a two-bedroom ranch exactly like every other house in the neighborhood. With a screened patio and a backyard full of iguanas.

Thunder Talking

T HE NEXT FEW weeks were difficult but rewarding in their own way. The act of dying was center stage, the day-to-day drama both real and surreal. The gloom it cast over everything was in sharp contrast to the brilliant light and sparkling tropical beauty of autumn in South Florida.

Yet there was a kind of comfort in the process. I had companionship. And my companions gave me the kind of reassurance I'd never had with a glass in my hand.

Mr Lasker's condition and, as a direct result, Vigo's and my moods, rose and fell throughout each day like the New York Stock Exchange. We rode the swells and dips together.

At the beginning of my stay, the market was flush: Mr Lasker rallied and I spent many hours by his side. Reading poems kept us both entertained. I'd brought an encyclopedia of classic British poetry and this compendium became one of our favorites. T.S. Eliot's *The Wasteland* was another.

Between coughing spells and naps Mr Lasker contacted former associates to say goodbye. I left the room so that he could conduct his affairs in private. The shaded alcove in the pool area provided me with a refreshing spot to take my breaks. Vigo came out to retrieve me whenever Mr Lasker wished for my company again.

One evening after we'd tired of Yeats, Lasker requested the phone. I handed it to him and got ready to leave.

"I gotta talk to Bobby G," he said.

My heart lurched around in my chest. I hurried off, my legs rubbery and weak. I hid in the pool house, stretched out on my bed in front of mind-numbing cable-TV news. I was hoping scenes of global violence would distract me from the acute desire to exert some local homicidal vengeance.

Sometime later I heard the unmistakable squeal of an expensive foreign sports car racing heedlessly up the driveway. I had given up on television and was lying on a chaise longue on the pool deck. I sat up.

Shit.

I'd been pondering the reality of the only true payoff in life. It was surely death, the ultimate end result – no matter how we lived our lives. After hard work, suffering and sacrifice, good people had to die. Yet, death was also the end result for the cheaters and scammers, scumbags and pedophiles. We all had the same grand finale, the same last chapter in our widely varied life stories. How fair was that?

I lay back again, closed my eyes. Bobby G had arrived? Who cared? I was tired of the whole setup. As far as I was concerned, the landscape of my life lay behind me now. Marnie? A lovely little pit stop on my pointless journey to nowhere. And there I had remained, alone, now with someone else about to leave me. Another person would soon die and leave me there, still stuck in my meaningless existence.

Vigo startled me out of my depressive reverie with a heavy hand on my shoulder.

When I sat up, he was already walking back toward the house, his shadow massive in the moonlight. He turned and waited, so I brushed the wrinkles from my rumpled shorts and shirt, then followed him inside.

I recognized the visitor in the great room. He looked as handsome and as untouchable as his newspaper photos. Bobby G, in the flesh. He stood beside Mr Lasker's bed, overdressed in a mint green double-breasted suit, a fuschia tie with a thick knot, and maroon Bragano loafers with tassels. The color scheme was Vegas meets Miami Beach. On acid.

My heart stuttered, the adrenaline spiking. Flight or fight? Easy choice. I didn't want to get killed by Bobby G. Not now. My life was pointless, but maybe a journey worth continuing after all.

Instinct told me to run. *Live,* my guts screamed.

I backed out of the room. But before I could turn and flee, high-tail it like a scared rabbit, scamper away to hide in the pool house, Mr Lasker spotted me. He raised an emaciated arm and waved it.

Shit.

He pointed to the chair by the bed, indicating I was to sit. Stay. Good dog.

My heart turned somersaults and the sweat dripped down my back. Bobby G didn't even look at me when I walked up and sank into the chair. I hoped for ongoing invisibility while my mortal enemy continued his dialogue with Mr Lasker.

Vigo came up and stood behind me, setting a reassuring hand on my shoulder. Mr Lasker sat propped by a mountain of pillows, his body covered from chin to toe in a fluffy rose-colored quilt. The fire licked at a couple of thick logs. Perspiration pooled in the crack in my ass.

"Sorry to see you this way, Uncle Milt. You been a good friend to me."

Bobby G's bark didn't go with his bite, his words squeaking out like they'd been squeezed through a wringer. He sounded like a talking piglet from the film version of *Animal Farm.*

"Hey, Bobby, I appreciate your friendship, even in these last days," Mr Lasker said. "I look at this fucking situation as accepting transactional immunity. I mean, I'm entering the big Witness Protection Program in the sky, right?" He barked a pitiable laugh.

Bobby peeked at his Rolex. So disrespectful. I wanted to jump up and grab him by the throat and squeeze.

"Listen, Bobby," Mr Lasker continued. "I have my funeral all planned and I've put myself in some of the best hands available in this part of the state. Not that you personally would need such assistance, please don't misunderstand. But when the time comes for anyone in your family, I suggest you consider the people I'm working with. Remember this name: Professional Grievers, Inc."

I froze in my seat. What the hell was he doing?

"Outta where? We have our own boys do that kind of thing. You know that, Uncle Milt."

When I looked up at Bobby G, he was staring down at me. The ice in his blood was shaken, not stirred, I was sure of it. I looked away, my heart jittering in its little bone cage.

"This thing is different, Bobby. This is a process, with a discreet professional to lead you through the last days. And then, after you get done with that, you're fucking guaranteed good attendance at the public events. Wakes, funerals. Shit like that. It's like stacking the final deck. And nobody knows. It's on the sly, because Professional Grievers, see, it's a legit business. No ties."

"Uh huh," Bobby said. He must've been waiting for the punch line.

"So the guy who runs the operation –" Mr Lasker began.

I shook my head at him. *No, don't,* I mouthed soundlessly behind my mask. He frowned at me, so I shut my mouth and stifled a scream.

"– I'd like for you to meet him. He could do good things for the family's image. You know, you got some image issues right now. With all the confidential informers, the crybabies, the rats."

He was referring to the new generation of mobsters, many of whom failed to prioritize family allegiance. Owing to the alterations in sentencing laws, organized crime was no longer the same honorable club it had once been. In fact, modern-day members tended to tell all in exchange for reduced sentences. They threw family members under the bus in order to secure immunity. And they were naïve, hoping to pave the way for a bestselling book and popular Hollywood film.

Wise guys weren't so wise anymore.

Mr Lasker said, "The old guard, guys my age and your father's, may God rest his soul, we're dying off. You boys coming up, you have very different career agendas than the men who brought you in. But the old guard, they still demand the respect men like us deserve. Even when we're dead."

The ego!

"I know what you're saying, Uncle Milt." Bobby G clasped his manicured hands behind his back. "All my uncles, they talk about how it was in the old days. These guys are itchy, they hate being on the sidelines. But they're too old, the ones who haven't died already, some of 'em in their 80s or 90s. Still, they want to go out with a fucking bang, you're absolutely right."

His smile was genuine, but there was nothing behind it warmer than thirty-two degrees.

My body shook gently, imperceptibly. My hands clenched in my lap. Vigo pressed down on my shoulders, steadying me.

Mr Lasker's red eyes shone. He, for one, was enjoying the moment. "Hey, I'm helping you help *them*, Bobby. I think you should remember this number. Professional Grievers: 1-555-DIE-EASY. Spread the word. I understand Big Toady's family used them a few months back. I'm telling you, the old guys will be fucking grateful when you bring this to them."

I attempted to signal Mr Lasker, giving him the international hand motion for *What the fuck are you doing?*

He ignored me. "The corporate head is a man you know through a mutual friend. A fine man, and a dear friend of mine. I'd like for you to take good care of him. He's here right now with us. Bobby, say hello to my man for grieving, Seymour Allan."

I almost fell over. Vigo kept me upright, but I could feel the muscles in my back twitching violently. My mouth wrenched itself into a rigor grin. Grateful for the mask hiding my feelings, I sat there, twisted up inside myself, a real freakshow.

Bobby reached down, shook my hand. The perfect gentleman. His skin was gatorish, leathery and cold. He grunted, and our eyes met. He was a handsome animal, but an animal none the less.

He said, "Tell me how I know you, Allan."

I was struck dumb as hatred and fear churned in the distillery in my gut, releasing a poisonous acid that went straight to my head. I couldn't formulate a response because I was busy trying not to keel over. I sat there, twitching like a fool.

All my life I've had a recurring dream in which I am attempting to run from a faceless adversary but find myself frozen in place. You may have had such a nightmare yourself. Many of us do, it's quite common. But in that moment, frozen in that chair, staring up at that face, I fell into the dream of my life. I fell in and I couldn't climb out again.

Mr Lasker shot me a look that could kill, if coming from someone with a hundred more pounds on his bones. "His girlfriend worked at one of your clubs," he explained while I sat there goggle-eyed, mute. "She died in a car accident on 95. Not so long ago. Mr Allan has been processing his own grief ever since. This makes him a very apt mentor to the recently bereaved and the grief-stricken."

The grandfather clock picked that moment to announce the hour, pealing multiple times. The after-hum filled my head. Lasker slumped lower on his starched white pillow pile. He was losing steam.

Bobby stared at me curiously, like you might examine your own turd. "Okay, yeah, I know who you mean. Nice girl. Beautiful girl. Great dancer. Had her own dance business I was helping fund. Damn shame. The fucking driver of the other car? Guy was a total degenerate. No license. Had three drunk driving citations. I didn't cry no tears when that guy was found dead down Hialeah."

His eyes flicked away. He'd flushed me away forever.

"So yeah, maybe I tell the old guys about these special services, Uncle Milt. Make the old guard happy." He took Mr Lasker's hand gently in his own. "Good to have our conversation. Now you rest yourself. Okay?"

Mr Lasker smiled a little before his head lolled and he dropped off into an exhausted sleep. Vigo walked Bobby G to the door. I sat there until I heard the sports car roar to life. The tires squealed. I wanted to leave the room, but something made me stay right where I was.

Guilt.

I'd sent Marnie to her death. Bobby G should've killed *me* instead of that drunk driver.

No matter what Mr Lasker had claimed in his pitch, all of my bedside and graveside grieving for other people's demise had not erased my own grief. All the *only ifs*, and *if I hadn'ts* still made me pine for the soothing blot I could only obtain with glass after glass of something bitter, hard, and strong.

"That Bobby G," Mr Lasker said suddenly. I looked up, startled, but his eyes were still closed, his body unmoving. He laughed softly. "He doesn't have any enemies, that guy. But his friends all hate him."

He slept after that, with me by his side. Was I really off the hook with Bobby G? Had I ever been on it? I had no idea.

After his nap, Mr Lasker had Vigo set up his speaker phone.

I was half-asleep in my seat next to the hospital bed. My eyes were tired from reading Yeats. My mood was as bleak as one of the poet's laments. My own pointlessness had been made crystal clear in the absence of any delusions of adequacy.

The call went through and, as soon as Mr Lasker said hello, I stood up. I was planning to go for a swim. I needed to wake up, rinse off the nervous sweat, clear my mind. Get ready for the long night ahead. But Lasker held up a hand for me to stay. So I sat back down.

"Jimmy, my friend. How's life in the islands?"

I closed my eyes. Not again.

I had no idea who Mr Lasker was talking to or why he wanted me to listen in. But I felt sure it would involve giving out my name and business information to another powerful and scary mobster.

More last-minute gifts from Milton Lasker. My heart lumbered around in its dark cave and I could feel my calves clench up.

"I'm entering the Witness Protection Program nobody ever returns from, Jimmy," Lasker joked.

Hardee har.

After a few minutes of cancer prognosis small talk, he acknowledged Jimmy's clichéd words of sympathy. Everyone says the same thing when they're on the receiving end of a death notice. After all, what can the living say to the dying that hasn't already been said before?

"I will miss you too, my friend. We had good times, didn't we?" Mr Lasker's eyes were dry, his tone all business. "Listen, I need you to do me a favor. There's this girl who worked for Bill. She's got a beef with Bill's old lady, which can mean problems with Big Toady's crew. This is unnecessary. No fucking good for anybody. I want you to intervene. Can you do this for me? I'd like the young lady to work for a colleague of mine in a business venture he's running. Something called Professional Grievers, Inc. Let me tell you about this thing. You're gonna love it."

I didn't bother to jump out of my seat to protest everything he was saying. Yvonne was barely speaking to me and she certainly wasn't up for working for Raymond. As far as I knew, she was packing her bags to head out to Greece or Bora Bora, or home to Massachusetts. Maybe she was already gone. Besides, I had never told Mr Lasker about Yvonne, or that I needed his help with the Manahans. In fact, I wasn't sure how he knew what he knew about

166

the awkward, perhaps dangerous position Yvonne was in with the Manahan family.

Raymond had seemed to know all about me. Mr Lasker knew all about my business and my friends' business. Why didn't *I* know more about myself?

Maybe because I'd been too busy feeling bad about my past mistakes to take an honest look at my current life.

Mr Lasker gave the guy the pitch. My pitch. There was nothing I could say so I said nothing. The muscles in my back twitched uncontrollably. I looked forward to stepping into the pool, the water slightly salty from the special salt chlorinator, the moon overhead a hazy three-quarters full.

"Remember that number, Jimmy. And don't wait to make an appointment either. Time escapes from us faster than we want it to," Mr Lasker said before he hung up.

"That old guy, Jimmy?" he said to me in a tired whisper. "Used to be a big deal, big man around New York. You could stare through that guy's eyes, though, right into his unexamined conscience. Like looking into a bottomless pit or up into an empty sky."

I nodded, but I wasn't sure what Mr Lasker thought he was doing. He certainly meant well. He was trying to help me. And Yvonne. Someone he knew I cared about. Even though I hadn't acknowledged that to myself. Or to her.

His mouth sagged and his breathing deepened. His eyelids drooped, his head dropped to his chest. He looked fragile as a newborn chick. Where was the source of the man's power, if not in the diminishing shell of his body? How could all that power, that unique energy, just slip away? Milton Lasker had lived too fully for his life to be nothing in the end, yet there it was: the truth. The end was the same for all of us. A drop into the void.

The end truth of all our wasteland lives.

Together, Vigo and I moved the pillows and lifted the

ht body, settling him flat on the bed. It was like re-
cardboard cutout on a game board.

Lasker opened his eyes for a moment. "I feel better now,"
he said. "Despite your low self-opinion, I see your real worth, Seymour. You're in touch with a part of yourself most people ignore.
The sad part, the deeply sad part. This is where we're all the same.
Where we're all one thing. It's meant a lot to me to understand
that. So I wanted to do something to help you, Seymour. To show
you I take care of my assets. My real assets."

He sighed and the air echoed in the empty cavern of his lungs.
He looked past me, past everything. Like he had moved beyond
it all.

Milton Lasker reached for my hand and I let him hang on for
as long as he wanted. For as long as he was able. His eyes fluttered
closed again and he whispered something. He spoke so softly I
had to bend down to hear the words.

"Got to appreciate your assets, Seymour. Then let them go."

I held what was left of Mr Lasker's hand until his breathing
deepened and his bony fist dropped to his side.

Vigo collapsed in the chair beside the bed. His face was wet.
I turned my own damp face away and collected myself. Then I
headed for the pool.

Mr Lasker slept through the night and all through the following
day. No coughing, no tossing limbs, no calling out in fevered
dreams. No phone calls, no poetry, no discussions or words of
advice. He looked so small and inconsequential, inert and paltry
as he lay there in the rented hospital bed. I was reminded of the
Seventh Rule of Professional Grievers: We all die in a shortened
bed with a narrow sheet.

Eventually, Vigo and I realized that Mr Lasker wasn't sleeping.
He had slipped into a coma. Finally, his time had come. He was
letting go of his life.

My assignment was coming to an end. The job was almost done. I felt relieved and surprisingly sad.

Milton Lasker's orders for this final phase of his passing had been explicit: no nurses, no hospitals, no last-minute heroics or resuscitation. An ease of transition as organic as what was once referred to as *dying of natural causes.*

There are perfectly good reasons why this method of transitioning from one state of being to another, that is, from beingness to nonbeingness, has decreased in popularity in the civilized world. Dying wholly unassisted by medical technology is messy. It can take an unbearably long time if there are no drugs to help the body systems reduce their automatic functions. This means caretakers must allow the dying to slowly starve to death, or they must wait helplessly while the illness itself gradually shuts down the essential organs. Caretakers have to step back and restrain themselves from any kind of intervention.

In other words, you stand by. You can't make the dying person comfortable. *You* certainly aren't comfortable. But you wait, dealing as best you can with your own and the dying person's discomfort.

Hospice can be extraordinarily helpful to those in the trenches with their loved ones. The hospice workers tend to some of the dirty work, they provide emotional support and professional guidance. But Mr Lasker didn't want hospice there at the end. He wanted us. Vigo and me.

It was like being at the scene of a terrible accident. You watch as the first responders arrive, the police and the fire trucks, and you can't tear your eyes away. You're fascinated by your own helplessness. Then the emotional weight hits you broadside and you want to get as far away as fast as possible. But you don't. You stay and stay. It's horrible, but you stay. Isn't there something you should be doing to help? How can there be nothing, *absolutely nothing you can do* to help?

Thus, the Eighth Rule of Professional Grievers: At the end, we sit helpless in a ruined house. No matter how grand the mansion or how beautiful the body, it's all the same in our last moments. There's the heart of it, the true meaning in meaninglessness.

Vigo resided in the southern wing of Mr Lasker's house. I had to venture down a long, thickly carpeted hall to a set of polished oak doors, where I would knock twice to alert him to his turn on duty. The suite had a massive waterbed, a marble bath with triple shower heads, and a living area packed with the best electronics money could buy. Vigo relaxed on a plush semicircular couch and watched ESPN. He also watched cooking shows. Vigo was a cooking savant. His soufflés were incredible. We shared meals during those long weeks of tending to Mr Lasker. Silent but relaxing, comforting meals.

We took turns tending to the dying man, trading off in four- or five-hour shifts. Even though it seemed to us as if our friend had already left the building. Like we were only housesitting, taking care of an empty mansion. A failing corporal home to which the owner would not be returning.

The days dragged on. Death was the one true thing. But it took its time getting there.

Watching Mr Lasker's body fail was overwhelmingly depressing. I wasn't a doctor or a nurse, certainly not cut out for that kind of work. You have to have a particular attitude toward the body and its numerous noises, its excretions. I would gag, on the verge of passing out from having to wipe up some odorous substance. I didn't have the necessary constitution for that.

Neither did Vigo.

One of us was always blanching, retching, or turning around and running from the room. This brought us closer. It was helpful to have a silent partner in my grief work.

Although he did not say so, I was sure Vigo felt the same way.

Fishing

THE THUNDER GREW louder with each contraction. The head of the storm was about to crown. It was so dark I could no longer see the shore. It felt as if we were entering a black hole, never to return.

I kept asking Raymond if we could head back. I begged him. He just laughed.

Raymond was high on the adventure. He stood at the helm of the thirty-foot Chris Craft, dressed in full gear. Bright yellow rain slicker, waterproof pants, black rubber boots. One of those collapsible hats decorated with fishing lures. I would've laughed at him if I wasn't so afraid of the blue-white zigzags of lightning charging the air around us and making my short hairs stand on end.

We were out on Palm Beach Lake. Which is, despite the fancy-pants name, a rather small, brackish basin between the Intra-coastal and the Atlantic. A lot of yachts hang out there. People of all ages on boats of every size swim or row or paddle over to one another's deck parties. Music blares from Bose speakers, and the booze flows.

But we were the only boat in the lake that day. Because the weather was only good for ducks. And we were sitting ducks, out on the water in the middle of a fast-moving storm.

We could've puttered over to the marina on the west side of the basin in mere minutes. We would've been out of danger, safe from lightning strikes before you could say "liar, liar, pants on fire." But Raymond would have none of it. He pronounced us perfectly safe and continued to ignore my pleas, casting and recasting his line.

Neither of us had caught any fish.

The excursion had been Raymond's idea. A way to get me outside my own head, he said. An activity to take my mind off Milton Lasker's slow crawl to death and the overwhelming fear I faced every morning when I awakened to find myself still living in the dying man's pool house.

Once again, I was trapped by the man who wouldn't let go of his life. What was left of it. He hadn't eaten in two weeks, he took no water, he was more shadow than man. All that was left was his comatose form. Vigo and I took turns sitting by the body, listening for the grandfather clock to chime the hour, a ring hollow in a room so empty of life.

"Raymond?" I pleaded when a bright bolt of lightning curved around in the shape of a horseshoe, arching directly over our heads. "Do you have a death wish?"

"Not for myself," he replied, then laughed. "Did you know more people die from lightning strikes in Florida than anyplace else in the world?"

My point exactly.

He reeled in his line so quickly I didn't bother to look. I was sure there was nothing on his hook except for the ground iguana meat he'd used as bait. I had earthworms on my hook. I hadn't felt a tug on my line all afternoon.

The weather had been beautiful when Raymond showed up on Mr Lasker's pool deck. I was on a break from bedside watch, snoozing in a fresh breeze off the ocean. The day was overcast and dry, not too hot, a refreshing change. It was the kind of day one might enjoy spending outdoors. Unless you are an experienced sunbather or an avid boater, the sun in South Florida is such a dominant force that hours outside can spell disaster. Especially when you reach a certain age and your skin reddens and shreds from even the mildest degree of UV abuse.

"What are you doing here?" was how I'd greeted my employer.

I was being honest. I hadn't called him, I hadn't expressed the desire to see him. I wasn't in the mood for socializing. My days were spent in total silence. I had grown accustomed to this in the company of the dying client and his speechless assistant.

I'd had a lot of time to think. But I still needed more.

Raymond smiled, baring his oversized teeth. "I'm here to provide you with a much-needed vacation from duty."

He was wearing pleated jeans and a freshly pressed white Oxford shirt. His leather boat shoes looked uncomfortably stiff, like he'd never worn them before. He looked stiff himself, as if he'd put on a costume to play a role.

I knew the feeling.

He removed his designer sunglasses so I could see his eyes. Impersonal eyes, drained of everything except that weird energy he had. But I could see he meant business.

"A fishing trip is what this doctor is ordering, Seymour."

I protested. "Mr Lasker needs me. So does Vigo. I only came outside for a short break. I can't go anywhere right now."

But I'd already given up. I had no choice. Raymond could take me off the case if he wanted to, it was his call. And, as much as I wanted the dying to be over, there was no way I would leave before the job was done. No way.

We took my car. Raymond said he had Mr Lasker's permission to use his fishing boat, which he kept at a private marina on the lake. Who was I to question him?

We climbed aboard and Raymond motored us out to the middle of the calm basin, where he dropped anchor. We fished for a few hours under soft grey clouds and it was indeed relaxing. But then the weather changed. Suddenly we were caught in the onrush of a real bully of a storm, with wind gusting at what felt like fifty or sixty miles an hour. I was woefully unprepared, still dressed in the light summer wear appropriate for sitting next to a roaring fire all day.

I shivered as cold blasts of damp air whipped in from the east. An ominous black cloud bank moved steadily closer. It carried within its massive billows the attractive energies for untold numbers of deadly electric bolts. Those lightning strikes would find us ready targets, unprotected out in the middle of the wind-driven lake.

My nerves were already frayed after the long weeks of death work at Mr Lasker's place. Now I felt sick. Not seasick, just plain sick.

Raymond checked his hook for a nonexistent fish. He looked over at me, then laughed like a madman. "You're green, my boy," he said, hee-hawing like I was the funniest thing he'd seen in years.

I said nothing. It was all I could do to keep my morning coffee from coming back up.

Wild scribbles of lightning brightened the sky, the thunder booming immediately after.

Moments later, I lost my breakfast coffee over the side of the rocking boat.

Suddenly, we were back on shore, sitting in my car in the lot for the marina. We were sitting there with the engine running, apparently waiting for a heavy deluge of rain to diminish.

I'd had a brief blackout. This reminded me of the months of excessive drinking after Marnie died. One minute I'd be standing over here, the next minute I'd be lying over there. And meanwhile *hours would have passed*. With nothing in between.

A world of nothing. A black hole. Like a taste of death.

I checked the car clock. We'd been gone for five hours.

The acrid taste in my mouth was familiar. The bitter taste of bile, coffee grounds, regurgitated alcohol. But I'd had nothing alcoholic to drink in weeks. Months, actually. Why was I having a booze flashback?

I stared at Raymond, sitting beside me in the passenger seat. He glimmered in the steamy car. His skin was so pale he looked see-through.

He looked like a ghost.

"Are you okay?" I asked someone, maybe myself.

Raymond had his eyes closed, his head back against the headrest. His body gave off a clammy chill. As I stared at him, he faded in and out of focus, dimmer and brighter, fainter, then more clear. His voice, however, was vibrant and loud. Too loud for the small confines of my car.

"In China, the peasants regarded a death in the home as a terrible curse. So they set aside special buildings for the dying. In the modern West, we have done the same thing but for different reasons. We remove the dying from our midst because we see their presence as a distraction from what is important. That is, making money, feeding the ego, indulging in our material pleasures. We move the dead and the near-dead out of the way to make room for the living. Only the living have a place in contemporary society."

He was no longer dressed in rain gear and his neatly pressed jeans and button-down shirt were dry. His hair was neatly combed, no wind snarls or errant locks. But I was sitting in a puddle of my own making. My clothes were soaked through and stuck to my goose-bump skin, what was left of my thin hair plastered against my skull. I was a total wreck. Raymond, on the other hand, looked perfect.

In fact, he looked a little too perfect.

So perfect *the man did not look real.*

Raymond flickered on and off, an eerie light in the gloom of the onset of early dusk. His voice filled my head.

"In Hawaii, a beloved person will inspire those he leaves behind to tattoo his name and the date of his death on their own bodies. On these beautiful islands, the native peoples are not afraid to become living tombstones: living testaments to the deceased they still regard with so much love and admiration. This is something we should consider more carefully here on the mainland, where we are ashamed of our dead. Where we are only too happy to hide our dying and all that they represent. Do you understand what I'm saying here, Seymour?"

"Raymond," I said sternly. "If you remember, *I'm* the one trying to spend time with Mr Lasker, our dying client. *You're* the one who dragged me here on this useless fishing expedition. I'm exceedingly grateful we didn't join the world of the dead ourselves just now. It's lucky we didn't get fried by lightning."

He didn't respond.

This pissed me off. "Are we done here? Can I go back to work now?"

The air we shared inside the car was weirdly thick and fuzzy. It smelled like overripe cheese. My nose was dripping so I fished for my handkerchief. It was damp, and it smelled briny.

I wondered, had I been making the best of my own wasteland? I thought not.

"If we fail to build our own lives, how will we die?" Raymond asked rhetorically. He was referring to the Ninth Rule of Professional Grievers: We build our lives daily, and in the same way build our own deaths.

Waste and void, waste and void, all right. Nothing but that.

Outside, tree branches thrashed loudly in the strong wind. All the windows were fogged up, but the rain had stopped pounding on the car roof. Raymond sat beside me, eyes still closed, silent now.

Time passed in a strange rush, and then it was gone.

I started up the car and turned on the wipers, drove carefully through the flooded streets toward Mr Lasker's place, Raymond silent beside me. I flipped on the radio and listened to Bruce Springsteen sing about Philadelphia.

It felt like I was alone in the car.

When we arrived at the turn to Mr Lasker's estate, Raymond switched off the radio. He said, "Do you understand about lightning? How the energy not only comes down to the earth from clouds in the sky, but also comes up from the ground?"

He paused while I dissected his statement for relevance. I found none. It seemed to signify nothing.

Raymond continued. "The world around us is full of bizarre connections, with links to unknown forces both seen and unseen. Some of these same forces connect the living and the dead. Love is like a beautiful body of water that conducts the connectivity from one state of being to another, from beingness to non-beingness. And back again. You may not be clear right now as to why I do some of the things I do, Seymour. But believe me, I've always had your best interests at heart."

His voice was lulling, like a familiar song. I peeked at his waxy hands folded gently in his lap. They looked like a couple of dead fish.

I was creeping up the driveway, sloshing the car slowly through some very deep puddles, when he said, "This will be my final visit to you, Seymour. You're on your own now."

Whatever. I nodded absently. My main concern then was getting Raymond out of my hair so I could dry myself off and go sit with Mr Lasker. I didn't want the man to die alone. To die without me there.

Like Marnie had.

I parked beside the murky fountain, which was overflowing with brown leaves and rainwater. The bowl needed a good cleaning. The whole estate needed one. Raymond sat quietly, his hands folded as if in prayer, his wax museum face expressionless. He shimmered in the late afternoon light.

In a strange, exceedingly frightening way, he did not seem solid to me. But this thought was so freaky I didn't dare put out my hand and try to touch him.

When he spoke again, his voice sounded amplified, filling my whole head at once. "*He who was living is now dead.* And vice versa. A line from Eliot, of course." He paused, then said, "Seymour, I want to thank you for the time we've spent together. It's meant a lot to me. I think you will see it's meant quite a bit to you, too."

He still wasn't moving or looking at me. It was really freaking me out. I said, "Okay, Raymond. Thanks for coming. I've got to head inside now and get back to Mr Lasker. Forgive me for running off."

I jumped out of the car and slammed the door. The adrenaline was pumping through me as I sprinted for the pool house to grab a change of clothes. My soaked shoes and clothing were so heavy I felt as if I was in one of those nightmares where you can't run, as if some strange force is pulling you back.

When I rounded the corner of the main house I didn't bother to look over my shoulder or wave or anything. I just kept going.

I left Raymond sitting there in my old Toyota, flickering on and off.

Knocking on
Heaven's Door

O N T H E M O R N I N G of the fishing trip I'd had an idea. I'd been thinking a lot about how comforting it was to have Vigo at the deathbed attendance with me. And how helpful it had been to have Yvonne by my side at the has-been celebrity's funeral in the little chapel on the beach. Like a good bottle of expensive wine, grief is something that is better shared.

Hence, my idea. I'd decided to tell Raymond he should assign grievers in pairs. The work could be accomplished more efficiently and comprehensively with two grievers on a case.

But then he showed up in Boca, and we went out on the lake and got caught in the lightning storm, and he grew unreal, fuzzy, ghostlike. So I forgot all about my idea.

Back from the fishing trip, I forgot about Raymond too. I had other things on my mind. Dressed in dry clothes, I hurried to the house. Was Milton Lasker still with us?

The air in the great room was muggy but not as hot as it had been. Vigo had let the fire die out. Mr Lasker didn't seem to be suffering from the cold anymore. Room and body temperature were no longer relevant for him.

What exactly *was* relevant, I wondered. Where was Mr Lasker in that moment, if he was no longer in his body? Was he hanging around his house or had he moved on to somewhere unimaginable?

I couldn't feel his presence in the room. But I couldn't *not* feel his presence either.

Vigo was asleep in the chair by the bed. He needed to take extra time off, a solid break like I'd just had. It would do him good. I had a sense of renewed energy. My head felt surprisingly clear.

As I approached the bed, the telephone rang. Vigo awakened with a start. Although playing receptionist was not part of my job description, nobody else in the room could do the job. So I picked up the phone.

"How's he doin'?"

I recognized the squeaky voice of Bobby G. Mr Untouchable.

My heart beat steadily, my nerves remained calm. My hand did not shake. "In a coma," I answered in a professional griever voice. My legs did not tense up and I stood my ground.

I stood my fucking ground.

"Listen," he said. "There's people who want to pay their respects. People who lost track of Milton Lasker after he retired. He didn't know it, but a lot of guys respected him for getting out of the business. Living a quiet life. You call me when the time comes. I'll take care of the invitations."

I said okay. What else could I say? Mr Lasker would be pleased, was what I told the man I'd hated with all my being, the all-powerful monster I'd been blaming for the pathetic downturn that had constituted my life since I fell for Marnie. Since I lost Marnie. Since Marnie died.

I didn't feel that way anymore. Now that my head was finally clear. Now that the truth was clear to me. And the truth of the matter was this: Bobby G didn't kill Marnie. He didn't take her away from me.

I didn't kill her either.

The drunk driver killed Marnie. And he was dead now, too.

Life goes on. Until it doesn't anymore.

After I hung up, I told Vigo to take an extra-long break. He nodded. Then he made the sign of the cross and kissed Mr Lasker's hand. He slid the yarmulke off his head, folded it and stuffed it in his pocket. As he walked away, I noticed his sweat shorts drooped from his bulky frame. He'd lost weight.

For the first time I wondered about Vigo's future. Who would take care of Vigo once he was no longer on Milton Lasker's payroll? A grown man unable to speak, a gentle man with the appearance of a heavyweight thug. Vigo would need an adoptive home with ancillary support of some kind. He couldn't live on his own, could he?

I drew back the heavy drapes and opened all the windows. I wanted to invite the night into the room. I wanted to feel the ocean's salt on my skin, smell the briny seaweed scattered across the wet sand. I wanted to hear the tide pulling at the shore, dragging it away bit by bit to distant destinations.

Mr Lasker and I, we needed to be part of the night.

I stretched a pair of latex gloves across my lumpy knuckles, pulling them up over my wrists. Then I stood over Mr Lasker. His skin had turned an earthy shade, ocher, as if he were made of dirt and stone. His rasping inhalations were lengthy, drawn out, sometimes followed by a gurgling sound. An underwater sound.

The energy that had once swept me along to fancy country clubs and exclusive golf tees, the energy I felt while accompanying him in the Mercedes, the wind in our wispy hair, or while sitting right here in this room reading poetry, talking philosophy or laughing at ourselves, that energy was no more. I could feel nothing coming from the body of the person who was no longer, in any real sense, alive.

I knew how I could hasten the process that had been all but complete for weeks now. Simply by squeezing closed his shriveled nostrils and holding the position for a minute or two, I could put an end to the gargling and drooling, the oozing and dripping, the ongoing wasting away of a just about dead body.

I could take away so quickly what little life there was left.

But I knew exactly where these thoughts were coming from. My own fear. Death can feel like too much truth for any of us to bear. If I hastened the process, I would be acting out of a desire to reduce my own discomfort. Watching my friend die was more difficult for me than it was for him. He was braving his slow climb up the steep bank to the shore of a new world. To watch him leave us for the unknown land, I had to be brave too.

This was my job as a professional griever, and I needed to do it. Get it done. Finish the work.

After I aspirated some excretions and mopped up some others, I removed the gloves and sank into the familiar comfort of the bedside chair. What an excellent piece of furniture. The contours of the deep seat with its comfy arms and well-positioned footrest cupped the body in such a friendly and supportive manner. I felt as if I could live in a chair like that without the need for a bed or couch. I imagined I could make love in the chair and not exert myself unduly.

Yeah, right. Who was I kidding? I was thinking like a man who had a lover. A beautiful woman who should be, if life were fair, with a much better man. A woman I could love without reason, a woman who would have no reason to love me back. A woman like Marnie.

But Marnie was deceased. Her body had checked out, her soul had left the building. She was nobody's girlfriend now, at least not in our dimension. She'd died a sudden, sad, shockingly premature death. But her death was not an uncommon one. Death is death, it takes us all in ways that can seem harsh and unjust. Life wasn't fair, and neither was death. The clear truth was, Marnie was gone.

But Yvonne was not.

She answered on the second ring, her voice husky with sleep. "I've been thinking about you, Seymour."

My heart leapt and twirled. "Where are you?"

"Northern Vermont, at my family's camp. Oh god, you'd love it up here. The sky is so dark at night, I'd forgotten how dark the world can get. You can see so many stars. And the air smells rich and sharp, it smells like Christmas trees. There are birds everywhere. Songbirds and geese, whippoorwills, loons. It's so different from South Florida. Serene. Natural. And quiet. Quiet and beautiful."

It sounded like a dream. One of *my* dreams. Mountains. Birds. A beautiful woman.

"Yvonne, look. We need to talk. I can come up there when my job here is finished. If you want my company, I mean. I won't be drinking anything harder than mineral water," I promised.

"I make terrific herbal teas." Her voice was kind, forgiving.

I was so grateful to her for this I got choked up. I let her talk and the sound of her voice soothed me, it held me up in the darkness. I closed my eyes and imagined looking out the window at all the stars pinpricking the night. Millions of stars. Beyond all the light we cast out from our cities and highways, shopping malls and suburban developments, the stars are still there, hidden in plain view: millions of stars.

She said, "I had a couple of interesting phone calls. I heard we may be going into business together at some point, Seymour. I'm liking the idea of redefining my life. It sounds good, like a good thing for us. And for others. So maybe we'll have a planning session when you get here." She paused and I imagined the smile in her eyes, her long legs crossed at the ankles, the heat of her skin warming the deep darkness around her. "The trees are amazing right now, the leaves all red and gold and that beautiful shade of burnt orange. The nights are cold, though. Do you think you might make it up here before winter sets in?"

"Give me a few weeks," I told her.

We weren't in love. Not yet. But I felt something. And for me, a lonely middle-aged loser, feeling something was enough. I took comfort knowing I was moving away from, not toward, that cold dark place.

The Tenth Rule of Professional Grievers: Time is a series of moments, and the briefest moments are what give life meaning.

After Yvonne and I hung up, Milton Lasker took a final noisy breath. A whooshing sound escaped his blue lips, a balloon letting out all the air inside it. His jaw dropped then, and when I reached out for his hand, the skin was already ice cold.

The old clock chimed, and I wept.

Dream Interlude II

THE SEA IS rough, clawing at the back of the beach, tearing off bites. The waves are grey and white and they froth up when they hit the shore. My telescope is cold to the touch, the lens gritty with blowing sand. And the stars? They're tumbling out of the blue-black sky, one after another. They fall toward me, but I don't flinch. It's a blue-moon meteor shower, visible for the first time in fifty years.

One night many years ago my mother led me outside our apartment in South Boston. We stood on the sidewalk in the cold wind, staring bare-eyed at the sky while she tried to teach me what she knew about meteor showers.

My mother was a teacher. She spent more than thirty years in a rundown high school classroom. She taught literature with passion and joy. While I was growing up she taught me about the life of the literate mind. How you could let go of the pain and pressure of the physical world and float off into another realm, a parallel world where problems were resolved by the end of each narrative or explained away with either fantasy or scientific fact. Where life had meaning and death was mourned or made sense of by others. Where grief was a kind of enduring love and everything had purpose and you could feel what it would be like to come to terms with all the truths in the world.

I loved my mother. I admired her, too. But she believed in the need for children to earn love. And somehow I'd failed to do so.

That was a long time ago. Right now I watch the shooting stars, make a few wishes. I wish for a woman to love, a beautiful woman who could really love me. Unlike my mother who loved her books and her life away from her family, far away in her classroom, inside her own head. Unlike my ex-wife who did not even like me, and who rather quickly found someone else more worthy of her love.

Dust from another time trails itself across the blank slate of the night sky. The surf pounds on the door to another world. I inhale the distinct seashore smell of clam beds and iodine. And a hint of night-blooming jasmine.

A voice behind me says, "The stars must look amazing through your telescope."

Marnie.

She didn't want me for my money. A good thing because I didn't have any. She didn't want me for my body, I'm not foolish enough to believe that. She wanted me for *me*, for my self. My real self, the awkward, intellectual, half-geezer self. The kind, decent self I shared with her because she deserved a kind, decent man.

And then I took that away from her.

All my life I had to work very hard at believing in something. To convince myself it wasn't all for nothing. My tendency for depression repeatedly reminded me that the sum of my accomplishments was smaller than I thought it would be while the sum of my mistakes was frighteningly large. Like stars in the sky, my fuckups were countless, making it difficult for me to get out of bed each day and carry on.

Still, there I was. Because I knew life was like this: the tide comes in, the tide goes out, sometimes softly on cat feet, other times louder and harder than one would think possible. Always, you can count on the tide to be the tide. No matter what mood it's in.

I couldn't make sense of my life. I couldn't end the suffering. The best I could expect of myself was to be decent. Kind.

I handed the telescope to the young woman and
through it for a long time. The wind was cool enough
bumps formed on her bare shoulders. She was incred
ful. And sweet. I wanted to drape my body over hers and shelter
her from everything outside of that moment, everything except
me. I wanted to be the telescope, cradled softly but firmly in her
small hands. But I didn't dare touch her in case my body melded
with hers and kept going, in case my body traveled right through
her and I woke up from the beautiful dream.

Suddenly she laughed. She pointed up at the huge sky above
our heads and turned to face me, her long sleek hair whipping
about in the wind. "Someone told me once that the purpose of
psychoanalysis is to help you let go of your delusional suffering
and explore the misery and ultimate doom of reality." She pulled a
strand of glistening hair away from her generous mouth. "The sky
is falling. Make a wish."

"*This* is my wish," I admitted. "This is it."

Eulogy

W HEN STEPHEN HAWKING announced he'd made an error in his calculations, that travel to other dimensions *was* statistically possible, I didn't hear about it. I was busy drinking myself to death. So I missed out on those headlines. I missed out on a lot of things. Years later, when I was sober and living in Vermont, a series of lectures in honor of the late genius was held in Boston at the Planetarium there. Yvonne knew how curious I was about such things, so she encouraged me to attend.

I wanted to go but I was worried about leaving her to handle all the work. Business was booming and often hectic, but she reassured me she'd be fine. We had a growing staff of dedicated professional grievers, and Yvonne was super organized and efficient. She convinced me to take a few days off and attend the lectures.

You're wondering why the existence of alternate realities and the probabilities of multidimensional physics interested me enough to take a week away from my beloved wife and thriving business. The reason was this: I was looking for possible explanations for the sudden appearance and equally sudden disappearance of Raymond C. Dasher, the founder of Professional Grievers, Inc.

He'd warned me the last time I saw him on the day of the thunderstorm. He'd said I wouldn't be seeing him again. I could barely see him then, even though he was sitting right beside me in my car. Which was weird as hell. Still, I didn't believe him. Not literally. I was exhausted, I was out of it from weeks of death work. That's how I'd explained away the weirdness afterward.

We'd talked once more after our fishing expedition. Briefly, on the day after Milton Lasker died. I was pacing around the swimming pool with my cell, depleted, ranting. Mainly I talked and Raymond listened.

"I know I'm supposed to maintain a professional distance from our clients, but the experience with Mr Lasker has really gotten to me, Raymond. It's moved me, affecting me more deeply than I expected. It's like I can't stop thinking about my mother, when she died. I wasn't there. I was in my own head, too busy with my own life. This has never bothered me before, but now I feel awful about it. Even though it was so many years ago. And my girlfriend, when she died? I wasn't there. You know what I mean? *I was not there.* I didn't feel anything but my own loss. I drank to forget her. Remembering her was too painful. And there are all the others, people I've lost track of, friends who may be dead now. I'm thinking about all those people and how much they meant to me at certain points in my life. And how sad I am to be alone, without them."

It felt huge, this grief for everything and everyone I had ever known and lost. Huge and very real.

I paced by frangipani blooms on spindly stalks in bursts of yellow and white. A scatter of the fragrant petals floated delicately in Mr Lasker's popsicle-blue pool. As I strode around the perimeter of the deck, the scene before me seemed abstract and surreal. Like a digitally hyped version of a Monet painting.

"But you're not alone," Raymond told me. His voice faded in and out, our connection faulty. "Death of someone close allows us to appreciate more fully what we have not yet lost. Death gives us the opportunity to rethink our lives and plan for the future. Perhaps this is what you will do, Seymour."

"That's *all* I've been doing," I admitted. "Listen, I'm sorry to have to tell you this, but Professional Grievers, Inc., may soon become busier than ever. And most of the new clients will be people you really should be afraid of, Raymond. People who have done some very bad things."

Raymond laughed. At least I think he did. Our conversation was drowned out suddenly by the loud approach of the Goodyear blimp. I looked up at the big airship as it cast its dark shadow over me, the swimming pool, the vast tropical yard. The blimp slowly motored past, a fat grey blob of a bird, a scar on the cerulean sky, and I watched it go by. The flashing lights on its belly invited beach-goers to happy hour at a local Honda dealership.

Fucking Florida. Waste and void, waste and void.

Raymond was saying, "I thought you knew that from the beginning, Seymour." He also said, "Everybody dies. Even the bad guys with the most toys. We all lose in the end."

After that, our connection ended. I couldn't reach him when I redialed. Eventually, I gave up.

I tried to call him again a few days later, right before Milton Lasker's standing-room-only funeral service. Arranged by Bobby G. But Raymond's office phone rang and rang. Of course there was no receptionist. I still didn't understand how he could run a business that way.

After the burial ceremony, which was very well attended, Vigo and I handed over Mr Lasker's house keys to his attorney. Then we drove down to Hollywood in the Mercedes. Mr Lasker had left me the car in his will. Vigo received a generous settlement, enough that I didn't have to worry about his expenses when I invited him to come live with me.

On our way to Emerald Day Village, we stopped by Raymond's office. Vigo followed me up the stairs. The door to the office was unlocked, as always. I called out as we walked in.

No response.

We crunched over a rather tall pile of envelopes and other junk on the floor beneath the mail slot.

The reception area was empty. Dust motes danced in the stray sunlight rushing in through the open door. The room was stifling, the AC turned off. The office smelled stale, eggy and rotten.

Vigo went back outside with his hand over his nose while I walked down the hall, trying not to breathe. I entered Raymond's office, hoping I would find some clue to his whereabouts.

Sun filtered in through the venetian blinds, casting bars of light on the grey carpet. Someone had removed the hurricane shutter but failed to open the window. The room reeked, like a nasty reptile had died in an air conditioning vent. Only the ceiling fan moved, clicking after each revolution. Raymond's office appeared frozen in time, still and stark as ever, the sparse furniture dusty, the desktop clean.

Except for a single manila folder.

I slid my hand across the smooth oak desk and flipped open the folder. A contract lay on top of a two-inch pile of papers. When I noticed my name, I picked it up and read it carefully.

Raymond had given me the business. According to the contract signed by him, I was the new president and CEO of Professional Grievers, Inc.

I sat down at the desk and read through it again. The contract leaving me the business was not notarized. There was no lawyer involved, no city license, no business registration. Nothing beyond Raymond's neatly typed records.

I examined the records, then paged through them again, more carefully this time. I recognized some of the names, I'd been to their wakes and funerals. Two inches of files, the records of Raymond's clients. The people who had hired his company to attend end-of-life ceremonies. Dozens of clients, each with Raymond C. Dasher listed as the sole acting professional griever.

No other employees were listed; there was no mention of me

in any of the files. Not in the Manahan file, not in the multi-page Lasker file, not anywhere in the paperwork.

Huh.

Eventually I would hire a private investigator to track down Raymond. Several thousand dollars later, I would give up. The PI, an ex-cop from Miami, apologized. He claimed the whole thing was bizarre. There were no leads. None. He said it was as if Raymond C. Dasher had never existed.

In the records of Professional Grievers, Inc., it was as if *I* had never existed either.

I didn't know what to think. Fortunately, we got so damn busy so damn quickly, I didn't have time to think about it all that much.

As soon as Yvonne and I got back from our honeymoon vacation in Vermont, Professional Grievers, Inc., went legit. We registered with city and state, then rented a bright downtown office, built a flashy website, and hired a perky young receptionist. We advertised locally, our services rapidly in demand from Palm Beach to the Keys. We handled each of our clients personally, individually, on a case by case basis.

With Vigo and Yvonne working with me, I was able to build the company. Professional Grievers, Inc., became a successful family business. I mean, it was the "families" that kept us in business. When a new client called, he or she might say, "A family member referred me." And that would be enough.

You may wonder if doing business with criminals bothered me. I wondered that too. For a while I reassured myself with the idea that Bobby G owed me, that his family owed Marnie. But this wasn't the whole truth. Plausible deniability was useful for only so long before guilt replaced it. On some deep level, I knew that, soon enough, the guilt would get the better of me. It always did.

Every now and then, however, I would stop what I was doing and think about Raymond C. Dasher. Lingering over a client record at my cluttered glass desk in my air-conditioned office, I wondered, who *was* he? He seemed inexplicable, like a vision or a ghost. Might he have come to me from another dimension? Perhaps he only appeared to those of us trapped down in the cold dark place, people needing a lift back into the harsh but warming light of everyday life. Everyday, every feeling, life.

Because of Raymond, I'd spent time with the dead and dying. With mobsters, alligators, murderers, dead dogs, and lightning bolts. A man who wanted to kill me, and later to save me from my own grief. A new friend, a new lover, business partners, a wife. These were the exact experiences I required so that I might come back to life. But I had to be terrorized before I would quit my half-life, leaving behind that unfulfilling existence in someone's else's version of middle-age retirement.

Some of us require life or death situations for the meaning of meaninglessness to become clear. Clear enough to step out of the shadows and live an authentic life.

A life worth grieving over.

But only later, when it's over.

Raymond never gave me more than I could handle. Some people say this is what God does.

So Professional Grievers, Inc., was booming, Yvonne and I were doing great, and Vigo seemed content. He'd adapted instantly to life as a professional griever. The clients loved him. Nothing like a strong silent presence at a funeral to make everybody feel at home.

The three of us had moved into a Key West-style townhouse Yvonne found online. Rent was reasonable and some of the rooms overlooked the Intracoastal. The iguanas were everywhere. Vigo bought them bananas and heads of romaine lettuce. I liked to sit out on the patio looking at the water. I'd hold Catcher in my lap while Vigo fed the feral reptiles. The virus had been vanquished globally and life was good.

But my conscience still worked overtime, and the guilt by association grew. Finally, after several incredibly profitable years,

Yvonne and I decided to move Professional Grievers, Inc., out of South Florida. We established a second office ten miles south of her family's camp in Vermont, and Yvonne moved up there to supervise the expansion of our business. We were looking at a new type of clientele, so Yvonne focused her recruiting on retirement homes and assisted living programs.

Vigo and I joined Yvonne after I sold the Hollywood operation to an investment firm in Boca Raton. Let them handle the hit men and hookers, the self-made magnates and caustic Ponzi schemers. Up in the Green Mountains we had a smaller client load, mostly elderly spinsters and widowers who'd outlived their friends.

People were in need everywhere. And Professional Grievers, Inc., was ready to fill that need.

Vermont provided clean air, mountain water, and thick forests of towering pine. My wife was gorgeous and smart, my friend Vigo a steady presence. Business was good, the clients deserving. I wasn't lonely or sad. In fact, I felt better than I ever had. My depression had disappeared and the guilt that haunted me most of my life diminished until it was almost nonexistent.

I liked the idea that we'd recreated ourselves in another place and time.

Like Raymond must have done.

The sun was shining when I kissed my lovely wife goodbye and took what I still referred to as Mr Lasker's Mercedes to drive down to the Hawking lectures. Heading south on the back road that led to the interstate, I rolled down the window and breathed deeply. I was looking forward to smelling the clammy iodine scent of the Atlantic Ocean once I reached the coastline of southern New Hampshire. I missed the beach. Most everything else about my life in South Florida, however, I did not miss in the least.

On a local radio station, Steve Earle was making love to his guitar. Overhead, a big black vulture perched on the flat top of a telephone pole. The clouds behind its head formed a kind of crown. He looked majestic, an animal being itself in all its innate glory.

My mind was clear, the spring sky bright blue, the air cool and sweet. My heart felt light and expectant. I had made myself a good life.

I felt a sneeze coming on. Pollen. I slowed down and pulled out my handkerchief just in time to catch the powerful sneeze.

They say you come close to death when you sneeze. I'm not sure if this is medically accurate. But in my case, this particular sneeze blew me to the doorstep of my death.

And then it happened. The door opened.

I only had one hand on the steering wheel and one eye on the road when the tractor-trailer truck appeared out of nowhere and rammed me from behind. Before I could do anything but register the sound of screaming metal and burning rubber skidding across asphalt, the car was spinning madly. It whipped into a guardrail, careening off and sliding back toward the overturned truck.

The huge semi lay there, blocking the road. My car hurtled toward the back end of the truck, which had popped open and was spilling oranges all over the asphalt. Fresh citrus splatted across my windshield.

I had to laugh. Oranges? Was this freshly squeezed orange juice a parting gift from Florida?

Only your own life needs you there for it to go on, was what I was thinking. At least I'd finally made the best of my wasteland, was my other thought as Milton Lasker's Mercedes smashed into the back of the overturned truck.

Blackness. The black hole. That's all there was. Apparently, all the coffee spoons had been counted.

Let me just interject this before I continue: we are all so wrong about the past, the future, even the present, it's like we're insane people in one giant, Earth-sized lunatic asylum. Warped by our preconceptions and distorted by our memories, all our so-called realities are completely illusory. Our entire life experience is like a bizarre dream in which we are helpless to change anything but our own outlook.

Let me tell you this, too: death is just the final helpless moment in a lifetime of helpless moments. The end truth in a lifetime of half-truths.

Pay attention, everybody. Pay better attention than I ever did, please.

His is the first face I see when I return to consciousness. The blackness ends and there he is: my old friend Raymond C. Dasher.

He is seated across from me in a noisy café that, upon closer inspection, appears to be more of a coffee shop. The overly air-conditioned room is crowded with round tables and clusters of chairs. Young mothers sit with one another, their babies in jazzy strollers. A crew of tattooed teenagers swap tall cardboard cups overflowing with froth. Here and there, isolated elderly folks slump in their Bermuda shorts and cardigan sweaters, support socks and plastic sandals. Oldsters drinking coffee alone, staring into space. A few mutter to themselves. Others are talking to their crossword puzzles.

A loud thunderstorm pelts hard rain at the foggy plate glass windows.

"Excuse me," I say to Raymond.

We're at a little round table for two. He's ignoring me, examining a crossword puzzle in the newspaper folded open between us. His grey Brioni suit is rumpled, which surprises me. His faded hair looks more faded, perhaps because it has thinned considerably. His white skin is almost translucent.

The man looks ghostly.

"Excuse me," I repeat.

He's still staring at the puzzle. He appears to be stuck on 5-down.

Outside the shop, a big clap of thunder sets off several obnoxious car alarms. The noise is loud, but for some reason it fails to annoy me. I feel strangely serene. I watch patiently as Raymond chews the eraser on his number two pencil.

Raymond must sense me staring at him because finally he looks up. I may be imagining it, but his steel grey eyes seem slightly more inviting, warmer, possibly more alive than I remember. He removes his glasses and pinches the bridge of his nose.

"Mind if I join you?" I ask.

The question is rhetorical. I already have.

What I'm thinking is this: *He who is living is now dead*. And vice versa. Only I don't share this thought with Raymond.

I glance down at the coffee-stained tabletop. I can read upside down. One of my many useless talents. Automatically my mind plugs in the word Raymond is seeking, a five-letter word for a satirical comedy with an improbable plot.

Farce.

A real stretch, but it fits.

That's the way life is.

Until it isn't anymore.

The Ten Rules of Professional Grievers

First Rule: We create our lives from one moment to the next.

Second Rule: It is not possible to be of any real use to others.

Third Rule: All our knowledge reveals the extent of our true ignorance.

Fourth Rule: We must make perfect our will.

Fifth Rule: We must remember the cornerstones.

Sixth Rule: We must forget about the dividends.

Seventh Rule: We all die in a shortened bed with a narrow sheet.

Eighth Rule: At the end, we sit helpless in a ruined house.

Ninth Rule: We build our lives daily, and in the same way build our own deaths.

Tenth Rule: Time is a series of moments, and the briefest moments are what give life meaning.

Adapted from T.S. Eliot's poem "Choruses from the Rock."

Acknowledgments

T HE FOLLOWING NON-FICTION books provided helpful information on the grieving process, cultural approaches to death and dying, and the American mafia:

Joan Didion, *The Year of Magical Thinking*. New York: Knopf, 2005.

C.S. Lewis, *A Grief Observed*. London: Faber and Faber, 1961.

Tim Farrington, *A Hell of Mercy*. New York: Harper One, 2009.

Nigel Barley, *Grave Matters: A Lively History of Death Around the World*. New York: Henry Holt and Company, 1995.

Nicholas Pileggi, *Wise Guy*. New York: Pocket Books, 2010.

Joe Pistone, *Donnie Brasco – Unfinished Business*. Philadelphia: Running Press, 2007.

Joe Pistone, *The Way of the Wiseguy*. Philadelphia: Running Press, 2004.

Jack Vitek, *The Godfather of Tabloid*. Lexington, KY: The University Press of Kentucky, 2008.

~

The Ten Rules of Professional Grievers and much of the philosophy it is based on was inspired by the work of T.S. Eliot (See *Selected Poems 1888–1988*).

The Louise Glück poem referred to – "Trillium" – appears in *The Wild Iris* (HarperCollins, 1992).
Prologue data is from *New Scientist* and www.physics.org.

~

Parts of this book were published in short fiction form in digital book format (Champagne Books, 2015).

Acknowledgments

This book has been a work in progress for some time now. In its first rendition as a short story, the fantastic workshoppers at Writers in Paradise helped me to see the potential for more. Tom Perrotta provided initial guidance to shape the novel and Laura Lippman gave me the confidence to pursue it.

As a short fiction romantic comedy, the story was edited by several digital publishers including Ellen and Cassie at Champagne Books.

Some very talented writers assisted as the story evolved into a novel – including Brenda Ferber, Debbie Fischer, Athena Sasso, Jade Bos, and Mel Goss. The Inkwell and Boca Raton Women Writers offered insightful feedback along the way. Editor extraordinaire Linda Bennett and QuoScript guided the manuscript into its final form.

I also wish to thank my brother, who initially inspired the idea while searching for a job at local funeral homes. And my deepest gratitude goes to James, who shares and respects the ups and downs of living the writer's life.